THE
ESCAPED
COCK

D.H. LAWRENCE

edited
with a
commentary
by
Gerald M. Lacy

BLACK SPARROW PRESS • LOS ANGELES • 1973

First published 1928.
Copyright © 1928 by
David Herbert Lawrence.
Second printing 1973

LIBRARY OF CONGRESS CATALOGING IN PUBLICATION DATA

Lawrence, David Herbert, 1884-1930.
    The escaped cock.

    1. Jesus Christ—Fiction. 2. Lawrence, David Herbert, 1885-1930.
I. Lacy, Gerald M., ed.
II. Title.
PR6023.A93E7 1973   823'.9'12   73-12739
ISBN 0-87685-171-5
ISBN 0-87685-170-7 (pbk.)

PREFACE

I first became aware of some interesting differences between the manuscripts and the published texts of *The Escaped Cock* while working in the Humanities Research Center at The University of Texas at Austin in 1968. The novel had always appealed to me, and the rather large number of extant manuscripts offered an ideal opportunity to study its development. Also a large number of unpublished Lawrence letters contained important information about the novel. The present volume is the result of the study of the manuscripts, published texts, and the correspondence.

I gratefully acknowledge the assistance of a number of people and institutions. Angelo State University graciously gave me a leave of absence which enabled me to accept a Visiting Leverhulme Fellowship at the University of Manchester for a year of research. I would also like to thank Mrs. Caroline Moon of the Iowa State Education Association; Mr. Kenneth Duckett of Southern Illinois University; Professors Warren Roberts and David Farmer of the University of Texas at Austin; Miss Marte Shaw of the Houghton Reading Room, Harvard University; and especially Mrs. Enid Hilton for her generous response to my queries. Miss Paula Casillas was indispensible during the preparation of the manuscript.

I owe a great debt to Professor Perry Gragg of Angelo State University and Dr. Keith Sagar of the University of Manchester for reading the first draft of the Commentary and making many helpful suggestions. This project would not have been possible without the invaluable interest and cooperation of Mr. Laurence Pollinger, Literary Executor of the Lawrence Estate. And as editor of Lawrence, I must be unique in having a publisher with such enthusiasm for D. H. Lawrence—I do not think anyone, including myself, was any more pleased about this book than John Martin of Black Sparrow Press.

Finally, of all those who have assisted me, named and unnamed, my greatest debt is to Seamus Cooney of Western Michigan University, and editor of Black Sparrow Press, who thoughtfully provided the Table of Variants. While all the vices are mine, much of the virtue in the completed manuscript is due to his tenacious editing and to his circumspect suggestions.

G.M.L.
San Angelo, Texas
May 1973

ACKNOWLEDGEMENTS

I would like to acknowledge my debt to the following institutions for the use of material from their Lawrence collections.

The Poetry Collection of the Lockwood Memorial Library, State University of New York at Buffalo.

The Department of Special Collections, University Research Library, University of California, Los Angeles.

The University of Cincinnatti.

The Harvard College Library.

Iowa State Education Association, Des Moines, Iowa.

The Sterling Library, University of London.

The Morris Library, Special Collections, Southern Illinois University.

D. H. Lawrence Papers, Charlotte Ashley Felton Memorial Library, Manuscripts Division, Department of Special Collections, Stanford University Libraries.

The Humanities Research Center, The University of Texas at Austin.

Beinecke Rare Book and Manuscript Library, Yale University.

A NOTE ON THE TEXT

The Escaped Cock was originally published by the Black Sun Press, Paris, 1929—the only edition until the present one published under that title. Subsequent editions, beginning with the Secker edition (London, 1931) and the Knopf edition (New York, 1931), carried the title *The Man Who Died*, a title for which, as I show in my Commentary, there seems to be no authorial sanction.

The text published here is based on a study of all the known manuscripts and early printings of the novel. It differs substantially from others available (such as the Heinemann and Knopf editions under the title *The Man Who Died*) in that it restores numerous passages of Lawrence's text extant in the manscripts but omitted in previous printings. A full discussion of the manuscripts, of the nature and extent of the deletions, and of the case for restoring them will be found below in the Commentary, sections VII, VIII, and IX.

The letters in the second section of this book are all published here for the first time.

The original short story version of Part I of the novel appeared in *The Forum* magazine, February 1928, and has never been reprinted before.

TABLE OF CONTENTS

The watercolor painting
reproduced on the cover is by
D. H. Lawrence

THE ESCAPED COCK

PART I

There was a peasant near Jerusalem who acquired a young gamecock which looked a shabby little thing, but which put on brave feathers as spring advanced, and was resplendent with an arched and orange neck, by the time the fig-trees were letting out leaves from their end-tips.

This peasant was poor, he lived in a cottage of mud-brick and had only a little dirty inner courtyard with a tough fig-tree, for all his territory. He worked hard among the vines and olives and wheat of his master, then came home to sleep in the mud-brick cottage by the path. But he was proud of his young rooster. In the shut-in yard were three shabby hens which laid small eggs, shed the few feathers they had, and made a disproportionate amount of dirt. There was also, in a corner under a straw roof, a dull donkey that often went with the peasant to work, but sometimes stayed at home. And there was the peasant's wife, a black-browed youngish woman who did not work too hard. She threw a little grain, or the remains of the porridge-mess, to the fowls, and she cut green fodder with a sickle, for the ass.

The young cock grew to a certain splendour. By some freak of destiny, he was a dandy rooster, in that dirty little yard with three patchy hens. He learned to crane his neck and give shrill answers to the crowing of other cocks, beyond the walls, in a world he knew nothing of. But there was a special fiery colour to his crow, and the distant calling of the other cocks roused him to unexpected outbursts.

"How he sings," said the peasant, as he got up and pulled his day-shirt over his head.

13

"He is good for twenty hens," said the wife.

The peasant went out and looked with pride at his young rooster. A saucy, flamboyant bird, that had already made the final acquaintance of the three tattered hens. But the cockerel was tipping his head, listening to the challenge of far-off unseen cocks, in the unknown world. Ghost voices, crowing at him mysteriously out of limbo. He answered with a ringing defiance, never to be daunted.

"He will surely fly away one of these days," said the peasant's wife.

So they lured him with grain, caught him, though he fought with all his wings and feet, and they tied a cord round his shank, fastening it against the spur; and they tied the other end of the cord to the post that held up the donkey's straw pent-roof.

The young cock, freed, marched with a prancing stride of indignation away from the humans, came to the end of his string, gave a tug and a hitch of his tied leg, fell over for a moment, scuffled frantically on the unclean earthen floor, to the horror of the shabby hens, then, with a sickening lurch, regained his feet and stood to think. The peasant and the peasant's wife laughed heartily, and the young cock heard them. And he knew, with a gloomy, foreboding kind of knowledge, that he was tied by the leg.

He no longer pranced and ruffled and forged his feathers. He walked within the limits of his tether sombrely. Still he gobbled up the best bits of food. Still, sometimes, he saved an extra-best bit for his favourite hen of the moment. Still he pranced with quivering, rocking fierceness upon such of his harem as came nonchalantly within range, and gave off the invisible lure. And still he crowed defiance to the cock-crows that showered up out of limbo, in the dawn.

But there was now a grim voracity in the way he gobbled his food, and a pinched triumph in the way he seized upon the shabby hens. His voice, above all, had lost the full gold of its clangour. He was tied by the leg, and he knew it. Body, soul and spirit were tied by that string.

Underneath, however, the life in him was grimly unbroken. It was the cord that should break. So one morning just before the light of dawn, rousing from his slumbers with a sudden wave of strength, he leaped forward on his wings, and the string snapped. He gave a wild strange squawk, rose in one lift to the top of the wall, and there he crowed a loud and splitting crow. So loud, it woke the peasant.

At the same time, at the same hour before dawn, the same morning, a man awoke from a long sleep in which he was tied up. He woke numb and cold, inside a carved hole in the rock. Through all the long, long sleep his body had been full of hurt, and it was still full of hurt. He did not open his eyes. Yet he knew that he was awake, and numb, and cold, and rigid, and full of hurt, and tied up. His face was banded with cold bands, his legs were bandaged together. Only his hands were loose.

He could move if he wanted: he knew that. But he had no want. Who would want to come back from the dead? A deep, deep nausea stirred in him, at the premonition of movement. He resented already the fact of the strange, incalculable moving that had already taken place in him: the moving back into consciousness. He had not wished it. He had wanted to stay outside, in the place where even memory is stone dead.

But now, something had returned him, like a returned letter, and in the return he lay overcome with a sense of nausea. Yet suddenly his hands moved. They lifted up, cold, heavy and sore. Yet they lifted up, to drag away the cloth from his face, and to push at the shoulder-bands. Then they fell again, cold, heavy, numb, and sick with having moved even so much, unspeakably unwilling to move further.

With his face cleared, and his shoulders free, he lapsed again, and lay dead, resting on the cold nullity of being dead. It was the most desirable. And almost, he had it complete: the utter cold nullity of being outside.

Yet when he was most nearly gone, suddenly, driven by an ache at the wrists, his hands rose and began pushing at the bandages of his knees, his feet began to stir, even while his breast lay cold and dead still.

And at last, the eyes opened. On to the dark. The same dark!

15

Yet perhaps there was a pale chink of the all-disturbing light, prizing open the pure dark. He could not lift his head. The eyes closed. And again it was finished.

Then suddenly he leaned up, and the great world reeled. Bandages fell away. And narrow walls of rock closed upon him, and gave the new anguish of imprisonment. There were chinks of light. With a wave of strength that came from revulsion, he leaned forward, in that narrow cell of rock, and leaned frail hands on the rock near the chinks of light.

Strength came from somewhere, from revulsion, there was a crash and a wave of light, and the dead man was crouching in his lair, facing the animal onrush of light. Yet it was hardly dawn. And the strange, piercing keenness of daybreak's sharp breath was on him. It meant full awakening.

Slowly, slowly he crept down from the cell of rock, with the caution of the bitterly wounded. Bandages and linen and perfume fell away, and he crouched on the ground against the wall of rock, to recover oblivion. But he saw his hurt feet touching the earth again, with unspeakable pain, the earth they had meant to touch no more, and he saw his thin legs that had died, and pain unknowable, pain like utter bodily disillusion, filled him so full that he stood up, with one torn hand on the ledge of the tomb.

To be back! To be back again, after all that! He saw the linen swathing-bands fallen round his dead feet, and stooping, he picked them up, folded them, and laid them back in the rocky cavity from which he had emerged. Then he took the perfumed linen sheet, wrapped it round him as a mantle, and turned away, to the wanness of the chill dawn.

He was alone; and having died, was even beyond loneliness.

Filled still with the sickness of unspeakable disillusion, the man stepped with wincing feet down the rocky slope, past the sleeping soldiers, who lay wrapped in their woolen mantles under the wild laurels. Silent, on naked scarred feet, wrapped in a white linen shroud, he glanced down for a moment on the inert, heap-like bodies of the soldiers. They were repulsive, a slow squalor of limbs, and he felt a certain disgust. He passed on towards the road, lest

16

they should wake.

Having nowhere to go, he turned away from the city that stood on her hills. He slowly followed the road away from the town, past the olives, under which purple anemones were drooping in the chill of dawn, and rich-green herbage was pressing thick. The world, the same as ever, the natural world, thronging with greenness, a nightingale winsomely, wistfully, coaxingly calling from the bushes beside a runnel of water, in the world, the natural world of morning and evening, forever undying, from which he had died.

He went on, on scarred feet, neither of this world nor of the next. Neither here nor there, neither seeing nor yet sightless, he passed dimly on, away from the city and its precincts, wondering why he should be travelling, yet driven by a dim, deep nausea of disillusion, and a resolution of which he was not even aware.

Advancing in a kind of half-consciousness under the drystone wall of the olive orchard, he was roused by the shrill, wild crowing of a cock just near him, a sound which made him shiver as if a snake had touched him. He saw a black-and-orange cock on a bough above the road, then running through the olives of the upper level, a peasant in a gray woollen shirt-tunic. Leaping out of greenness, came the black-and-orange cock with the red comb, his tail-feathers streaming lustrous.

"O stop him, Master!" called the peasant. "My escaped cock!"

The man addressed, with a sudden flicker of life, opened his great white wings of a shroud in front of the leaping bird. The cock fell back with a squawk and a flutter, the peasant jumped forward, there was a terrific beating of wings, and whirring of feathers, then the peasant had the escaped cock safely under his arm, its wings shut down, its face crazily craning forward, its round eye goggling from its white chops.

"It's my escaped cock!" said the peasant, soothing the bird with his left hand, as he looked perspiringly up into the face of the man wrapped in white linen.

The peasant changed countenance, and stood transfixed, as he looked into the dead-white face of the man who had died. That dead-white face, so still, with the black beard growing on it as if in

17

death; and those wide-open, black, sombre eyes, that had died; and those washed scars on the waxy forehead! The slow-blooded man of the fields let his jaw drop, in childish inability to meet the situation.

"Don't be afraid," said the man in the shroud. "I am not dead. They took me down too soon. So I have risen up. Yet if they discover me, they will do it all over again . . . ."

He spoke in a voice of old disgust. Humanity! Especially humanity in authority! There was only one thing it could do. He looked with black, indifferent eyes into the quick, shifty eyes of the peasant. The peasant quailed, and was powerless under the look of deathly indifference, and strange, cold resoluteness. He could only say the one thing he was afraid to say:

"Will you hide in my house, Master?"

"I will rest there. But if you tell anyone, you know what will happen. You too will have to go before a judge."

"Me! I shan't speak! Let us be quick!"

The peasant looked round in fear, wondering sulkily why he had let himself in for this doom. The man with scarred feet climbed painfully up to the level of the olive garden, and followed the sullen, hurrying peasant across the green wheat among the olive trees. He felt the cool silkiness of the young wheat under his feet that had been dead, and the roughishness of its separate life was apparent to him. At the edges of rocks he saw the silky, silvery-haired buds of the scarlet anemone bending downwards; and they too were in another world. In his own world he was alone, utterly alone. These things around him were in a world that had never died. But he himself had died, or had been killed from out of it, and all that remained now was the great void nausea of utter disillusion.

They came to a clay cottage, and the peasant waited dejectedly for the other man to pass.

"Pass!" he said. "Pass! We have not been seen."

The man in white linen entered the earthen room, taking with him the aroma of strange perfumes. The peasant closed the door, and passed through the inner doorway to the yard, where the ass stood within the high walls, safe from being stolen. There the peasant, in great disquietude, tied up the cock. The man with the waxen face sat down on a mat near the hearth, for he was spent and barely conscious. Yet he heard outside the whispering of the peasant to his wife, for the woman had been watching from the roof.

Presently they came in, and the woman hid her face. She poured water, and put bread and dried figs on a wooden platter.

"Eat, Master!" said the peasant. "No one has seen. Eat!"

But the stranger had no desire for food. Yet he moistened a little bread in the water, and ate it, since life must be. But desire was dead in him, even for food and drink. He had risen without desire, without even the desire to live, empty save for the all-overwhelming disillusion that lay like nausea where his life had been. Yet perhaps, deeper even than disillusion, was a desireless resoluteness, deeper even than consciousness.

The peasant and his wife stood near the door, watching. They saw with terror the livid wounds on the thin, waxy hands and the thin feet of the stranger, and the small lacerations in his still-dead forehead. They smelled with terror the scent of rich perfumes that came from him, from his body. And they looked at the fine, snowy, costly linen. Perhaps really he was a dead king, from the region of terrors. And he was still cold and remote in the region of death, with perfumes coming from his transparent body as if from some strange flower.

Having with difficulty swallowed some of the moistened bread, he lifted his eyes to them. He saw them as they were: limited, meagre in their life, without any splendour of gesture and of courage. But they were what they were, slow inevitable parts of the natural world. They had no nobility, but fear made them willing to serve.

And the stranger had compassion on them again, for he knew that they would respond best to gentleness, giving back a clumsy service again.

"Do not be afraid," he said to them quietly. "Let me stay a little while with you. I shall not stay long. And when I go away you will be paid. But do not be afraid. No harm will come to you through me."

They believed him really, yet the fear did not leave them. And they said:

"Stay, Master, while ever you will. Rest! Rest quietly!"

But they were afraid.

So he let them be, and the peasant went away with the ass. The sun had risen bright, and in the dark house with the door shut the man was again as if in the tomb. So he said to the woman:

"I would lie in the yard."

And she swept the yard for him, and laid him a mat, and he lay down under the wall in the morning sun. There he saw the first green leaves spurting like flames from the ends of the enclosed fig-tree, out of the bareness to the sky of spring above. But the man who had died could not look, he only lay quite still in the sun which was not yet too hot, and had no desire in him, not even to move. But he lay with his thin legs in the sun, his black, perfumed hair falling into the hollows of his neck, and his thin, colourless arms utterly inert. As he lay there the hens clucked and scratched, and the escaped cock, caught and tied by the leg again, cowered in a corner.

The peasant woman was frightened. She came peeping, and seeing him never move, feared to have a dead man in the yard. But the sun had grown stronger, he opened his eyes and looked at her. And now she was frightened of the man who was alive, but spoke nothing.

He opened his eyes, and saw the world again bright as glass. It was life, in which he had no share any more. But it shone outside him, blue sky, and a bare fig-tree with little jets of green leaf. Bright as glass, and he was not of it, for desire had failed.

Yet he was there, and not extinguished. The day passed in a kind of coma, and at evening he went into the house. The peasant man came home, but he was frightened, and had nothing to say. The stranger too ate of the mess of beans, a little. Then he washed his hands and turned to the wall, and was silent. The peasants were silent too. They watched their guest sleep. Sleep was so near death, he could still sleep.

Yet when the sun came up, he went again to lie in the yard. The sun was the one thing that drew him and swayed him, and he still wanted to feel the cool air of morning in his nostrils, and the pale sky overhead. He still hated to be shut up.

As he came out, the young cock crowed. It was a diminished, pinched cry, but there was that in the voice of the bird stronger than chagrin. It was the necessity to live, and even to cry out the triumph of life. The man who had died stood and watched the cock who had escaped and been caught, ruffling himself up, rising forward on his toes, throwing up his head and parting his beak in another challenge from life to death. The brave sounds rang out, and though they were diminished by the cord round the bird's leg, they were not cut off. The man who had died looked nakedly on-to life, and saw a vast resoluteness everywhere flinging itself up in stormy or subtle wave-crests, foam-tips emerging out of the blue invisible, a black-and-orange cock, or the green flame tongues out of the extremes of the fig-tree. They came forth, these things and creatures of spring, glowing with desire and with assertion. They came like crests of foam, out of the blue flood of the invisible de-sire, out of the vast invisible sea of strength, and they came col-oured and tangible, evanescent, yet deathless in their coming. The man who had died looked on the great swing into existence of things that had not died, but he saw no longer their tremulous de-sire to exist and to be. He heard instead their ringing, ringing, de-fiant challenge to all other things existing. The man lay still, with eyes that had died now wide open and darkly still, seeing the ever-lasting resoluteness of life. And the cock, with a flat, brilliant glance, glanced back at him, with a bird's half-seeing look. And always, the man who had died saw not the bird alone, but the short, sharp wave of life of which the bird was the crest. He watched the queer, beaky motion of the creature as it gobbled into itself the scraps of food; its glancing of the eye of life, ever alert and watch-ful, overweening and cautious, and the voice of its life, crowing triumph and assertion, yet strangled by a cord of circumstance. He seemed to hear the queer speech of very life, as the cock trium-phantly imitated the clucking of the favourite hen, when she had laid an egg, a clucking which still had, in the male bird, the hollow chagrin of the cord round his leg. And when the man threw a bit of bread to the cock, it called with an extraordinary cooing tenderness, tousling and saving the morsel for the hens. The hens ran up greedily, and carried the morsel away beyond the reach of the string.

Then, walking complacently after them, suddenly the male bird's leg would hitch at the end of his tether, and he would yield with a kind of collapse. His flag fell, he seemed to diminish, he would huddle in the shade. And he was young, his tail-feathers, glossy as they were, were not fully grown.

It was not till evening again that the tide of life in him made him forget. Then when his favourite hen came strolling unconcernedly near him, emitting the lure, he pounced on her with all his feathers vibrating. And the man who had died watched the unsteady, rocking vibration of the bent bird, and it was not the bird he saw, but one wave-tip of life overlapping for a minute another, in the tide of the swaying ocean of life. And the destiny of life seemed more fierce and compulsive to him even than the destiny of death. The doom of death was a shadow, compared to the raging destiny of life, the determined surge of life.

At twilight, the peasant came home with the ass, and he said:

"Master! It is said that the body was stolen from the garden, and the tomb is empty, and the soldiers are taken away, accursed Romans! And the women are there to weep."

The man who had died looked at the man who had not died.

"It is well," he said. "Say nothing, and we are safe."

And the peasant was relieved. He looked rather dirty and stupid, and even as much flaminess as that of the young cock, which he had tied by the leg, would never glow in him. He was without fire. But the man who had died thought to himself: Why then should he be lifted up? Clods of earth are turned over for refreshment; they are not to be lifted up. Let the earth remain earthy, and hold its own against the sky. I was wrong to seek to lift it up. It was wrong to try to interfere. The ploughshare of devastation will be set in the soil of Judaea, and the life of this peasant will be overturned

22

like the sods of the field. No man can save the earth from tillage. It is tillage, not salvation . . . .

So he saw the man, the peasant, with calm eyes; but the man who had died no longer wished to interfere in the soul of the man who had not died, and who could never die, save to return to earth. Let him return to earth in his own good hour, and let no one try to interfere, when the earth claims her own.

So the man with scars let the peasant go from him, for the peasant had no re-birth in him. Yet the man who had died said to himself: He is my host.

And at dawn, when he was better, the man who had died rose up, and on slow, sore feet retraced his way to the garden. For he had been betrayed in a garden, and buried in a garden. And as he turned round the screen of laurels, near the rock-face, he saw a woman hovering [close] to the tomb, a woman in blue and yellow. She peeped again into the mouth of the hole, that was like a deep cupboard. But still there was nothing. And she wrung her hands and wept. And as she turned away, she saw the man in white, standing by the laurels, and she gave a cry, thinking it might be a spy, and she said:

"They have taken him away!"

So he said to her:

"Madeleine!"

Then she went pale as if she would fall, for she knew him. And he said to her:

"Madeleine! Do not be afraid. I am alive. They took me down too soon, so I came back to life. Then I was sheltered in a house."

She did not know what to say, but fell at his feet, to kiss them.

"Don't touch me, Madeleine," he said. "Not yet! I am not yet healed and in touch with men."

So she wept, because she did not know what to do. And he said:

"Let us go aside, among the bushes, where we can speak unseen."

So in her blue mantle and her yellow robe, she followed him among the trees, and he sat down under a myrtle bush. And he said:

"I am not yet quite come to. Madeleine, what is to be done

23

next?"

"Master!" she said. "Oh, we have wept for you! And will you come back to us?"

"What is finished is finished, and for me the end is past," he said. "The stream will run till no more rains fill it, then it will dry up. For me that life is over."

"And will you give up your triumph?" she said sadly.

"My triumph," he said, "is that I am not dead. I have outlived my mission, and know no more of it. It is my triumph. I have survived the day and the death of my interference, and am still a man. I am young still, Madeleine, not even come to middle age. I am glad all that is over. It had to be. But now I am glad it is over, and the day of my interference is done. The teacher and the saviour are dead in me; now I can go about my own business, into my own single life."

She heard him, and did not fully understand. But what he said made her feel disappointed.

"But you will come back to us?" she said, insisting.

"I don't know what I shall do," he said. "When I am healed, I shall know better. But my mission is over, and my teaching is finished, and death has saved me from my own salvation. Oh Madeleine, I want to take my single way in life, which is my portion. My public life is over, the life of my conviction and my mission, the life of my self-importance. Now I can wait on life, and say nothing, and have no one betray me. I wanted to be greater than the limits of my hands and feet, so I brought betrayal on myself. And I know I wronged Judas, my poor Judas. Now I know. He died as I died, my poor Judas. For I have died, and now I know my own limits. Now I can live without striving to sway others any more. For my reach ends in my finger-tips, and my stride is no longer than the ends of my toes. Yet I would embrace multitudes, I who have never truly embraced even one woman, or one man. But Judas and the high priests delivered me from my own salvation, and I am no longer a lover of multitudes."

"Do you want to be alone henceforward?" she asked. "And was your mission nothing? Was it all untrue?"

"Nay," he said. "Neither were your lovers in the past nothing. They were much to you, but you took more than you gave. Then you came to me for salvation from your own excess. And I, in my mission, I too ran to excess. I gave more than I took, and that also is woe, and vanity. So Judas and the high priests snatched me from my own excessive giving. Don't run to excess now in giving, Madeleine. It only means another death."

She pondered bitterly, for the need for excessive giving was in her, and she could not bear to be denied.

"And will you not come back to us?" she said. "Have you risen for yourself alone?"

He heard the sarcasm in her voice, and looked at her beautiful face, which still was dense with excessive need for salvation from the woman she had been, the female who had caught men with her will. The cloud of necessity was on her, to be saved from the old, greedy self, who had embraced many men, and taken more than she gave. Now the other doom was on her. She wanted to give without taking. And that too is vicious, and cruel to the warm body.

"I have not risen from the dead in order to seek death again," he said.

She glanced up at him, and saw the weariness settling again on his waxy face, and the vast disillusion in his dark eyes, and the underlying indifference. He felt her glance, and said to himself: Now my own followers will want to do me to death again, for having risen up different from their expectation.

"But you will come to us, to see us, us who love you?" she said.

He laughed a little, and said:

"Ah yes!" Then he added, "Have you a little money? Will you give me a little money? I owe it."

She had not much, but it pleased her to give it to him.

"Do you think," he said to her, "that I might come and live with you in your house?"

She looked up at him with large blue eyes, that gleamed strangely.

"Now?" she said, with peculiar triumph.

And he, who shrank now from triumph of any sort, his own or

another's, said:

"Not now! Later, when I am healed, and . . . and I am in touch with the flesh."

The words faltered in him. And in his heart, he knew he would never go to live in her house. For the flicker of triumph had gleamed in her eyes: the greed of giving. But she murmured, in a humming rapture:

"Ah, you know I would give up everything to you."

"Nay!" he said. "I didn't ask that."

A revulsion from all the life he had known came over him again, the great nausea of disillusion, and the spear-thrust through his bowels. He crouched under the myrtle bushes, without strength. Yet his eyes were open. And she looked at him again, and she saw that it was not the Messiah. The Messiah had not risen. This was just a man. The enthusiasm and the burning purity were gone, and the rapt youth. His youth was dead. This man was middle-aged and disillusioned, with a certain terrible indifference, and a resoluteness which love would never conquer. This was not the Master she had so adored, the young, flamy, unphysical exalter of her soul. This was nearer to the lovers she had known of old, but with a greater indifference to the personal issue, and a lesser susceptibility.

She was thrown out of the balance of her rapturous, anguished adoration. This risen man was the death of her dream.

"You should go now," he said to her. "Do not touch me, I am in death. I shall come again, here, on the third day. Come, if you will, at dawn. And we will speak again."

She went away, perturbed and shattered. Yet as she went, her mind discarded the bitterness of the reality, and she conjured up rapture and wonder, that the Master was risen and was not dead. He was risen, the Saviour, the exalter, the wonder-worker! He was risen, but not as man; as pure God, who should not be touched by flesh, and who should be rapt away into Heaven. It was the most glorious and most ghostly of the miracles.

Meanwhile the man who had died gathered himself together at last, and slowly made his way to the peasant's house. He was glad to go back to them, and away from Madeleine and his own associates. For the peasants had the inertia of earth, and would let him rest, and as yet, would put no compulsion on him.

The woman was on the roof, looking for him. She was afraid that he had gone away. His presence in the house had become like gentle wine to her. She hastened to the door, to him.

"Where have you been, Master?" she said. "Why did you go away?"

"I have been to walk in a garden, and I have seen a friend, who gave me a little money. It is for you."

He held out his thin hand, with the small amount of money, all that Madeleine could give him. The peasant's wife's eyes glistened, for money was scarce, and she said:

"Oh, Master! And is it truly mine?"

"Take it!" he said. "It buys bread, and bread brings life."

So he lay down in the yard again, sick with relief at being alone again. For with the peasants he could be alone, but his own friends would never let him be alone. And in the safety of the yard, the young cock was dear to him, as it shouted in the helpless zest of life, and finished in the helpless humiliation of being tied by the leg. This day the ass stood swishing her tail under the shed. The man who had died lay down, and turned utterly away from life, in the sickness of death in life.

But the woman brought wine and water, and sweetened cakes, and roused him, so that he ate a little, to please her. The day was hot, and as she crouched to serve him, he saw her breasts sway from her humble body, under her smock. He knew she wished he would desire her, and she was youngish, and not unpleasant. And he, who had never known a woman, would have desired her if he could. But he could not want her, though he felt troubled by her soft, crouching, humble body. But it was her thoughts, her consciousness, he could not mingle with. She was pleased with the money, and now she wanted to take more from him. She wanted the embrace of his body. But her little soul was hard, and short-sighted, and grasping, her body had its little greed, and no gentle reverence of the return gift. So he spoke a quiet, courteous word to her, and turned away.

Risen from the dead, he had realised at last that the body, too, has its little life, and beyond that, the greater life. He was virgin, in recoil from the little, greedy life of the body. But now he knew that virginity is a form of greed; and the body rises again to give and to take, to take and to give, ungreedily. Now he knew that he had risen for the greater life of the body, not greedy to give, not greedy to take, but moving towards the living being with whom he could mingle his body. Now, having died, he was patient, knowing there was time, an eternity of time. And he was driven by no greedy desire, either to give himself to others, or to grasp anything for himself. For he had died. And he knew how rare was the risen body, the twice-born limbs rare, rarer far than the twice-born spirit, which could house in greedy flesh.

The peasant came home from work, and said:

"Master, I thank you for the money. But we did not want it. And all I have is yours."

But the man who had died was sad, because the peasant stood there in the little, greedy body, and his eyes were cunning and sparkling with the hope of greater rewards in money, later on. True, the peasant had taken him in free, and had *risked* getting no reward. But the will was cunning in him. Yet even this was as men are made. So when the peasant would have helped him to rise, for night had fallen, the man who had died said:

"Don't touch me, brother. I am not yet risen to the Father."

The sun burned with greater splendour, and burnished the young cock brighter. But the peasant kept the string renewed, and the bird was a prisoner. Yet the flame of life burned up to a sharp point in the cock, so that it eyed askance and haughtily the man who had died. And the man smiled, and held the bird dear, and he said to it: Surely thou art risen to the Father, among birds.— And the young cock, answering, crowed.

When at dawn on the third morning the man went to the garden, he was absorbed, thinking of the greater life of the body, beyond the little, narrow, greedy life. So he came through the thick screen of laurel and myrtle bushes, near the rock, suddenly, and he saw three women near the tomb. One was Madeleine, and one was the woman who had been his mother, and the third was a woman he knew, called Joan. He looked up and saw them all, and they saw him, and they were all afraid.

He stood arrested in the distance, knowing they were there to claim him back, bodily. But he would in no wise return to them. Pallid, in the shadow of a grey morning that was blowing to rain, he saw them and turned away. But Madeleine hastened towards him.

"I did not bring them," she said. "They have come of themselves. See, I have brought you money!—Will you not speak to them?"

She offered him some gold pieces, and he took them, saying:

"May I have this money? I shall need it!—I cannot speak to them, for I am not yet ascended to the Father.—And I must leave you now."

"Ah! Where will you go?" she cried.

He looked at her, and saw she was clutching for the man in him who had died and was dead, the man of his youth and his mission, of his chastity and his fear, of his little life, his giving without taking.

"I must go to my Father!" he said.

"And you will leave us?—There is your mother!" she cried, turning round with the old anguish, which yet was sweet to her.

"But now I must ascend to my Father," he said, and he drew back into the bushes, and so turned quickly and went away, saying to himself: Now I belong to no one, and have no connection, and my mission or gospel is gone from me. Lo! I cannot make even my own life, and what have I to save? I can learn to be alone.

So he went back to the peasant's house, to the yard where the young cock was tied by the leg, with a string. And he wanted no one, for it was best to be alone; for the presence of people made him lonely. The sun and the subtle salve of spring healed his wounds, even the gaping wound of disillusion through his bowels was closing up. And his need of men and women, his fever to save them and to be saved by them, this too was healing in him. Whatever came of touch between himself and the race of man, henceforth, should come without trespass or compulsion. For he said to himself: I tried to compel them to live, so they compelled me to die. It is always so, with compulsion. The recoil kills the advance. Now is my time to be alone.

Therefore he went no more to the garden, but lay still and saw the sun, or walked at dusk across the olive slopes, among the green wheat, that rose a palm-breadth higher every sunny day. And always he thought to himself: How glad I am, to have fulfilled my mission, and to be beyond it! Now I can be alone, and leave all things to themselves, and the fig-tree may be barren if it will, and the rich may be rich. My way is my own alone.

So the green jets of leaves unspread on the fig-tree, with the bright, translucent green blood of the tree. And the young cock grew brighter, more lustrous with the sun's burnishing; yet always tied by the leg with a string. And the sun went down more and more in pomp, out of the gold and red-flushed air. The man who had died was aware of it all, and he thought: The Word is but the midge that bites at evening. Man is tormented with words like midges, and they follow him right into the tomb. But beyond the tomb they cannot go. Now I have passed the place where words can bite, and the air is clear, and there is nothing to say, and I am alone within my own skin, which is the walls of all my domain.

So he healed of his wounds, and enjoyed his immortality of being alive without fret. For in the tomb he had slipped that noose, which we call care. For in the tomb he had left his striving self, which cares and asserts itself. Now his uncaring self healed and became whole within his skin, and he smiled to himself with pure aloneness, which is one sort of immortality.

Then he said to himself: I will wander the earth, and say nothing. For nothing is so marvellous as to be alone in the phenomenal world, which is raging and yet apart. And I have not seen it, I was too much blinded by my confusion within it. Now I will wander among the stirring of the phenomenal world, for it is the stirring of all things among themselves which leaves me purely alone.

So he communed with himself, and decided to be a physician. Because the power was still in him, to heal any man or child who touched his compassion. Therefore he cut his hair and his beard after the right fashion, and moved slowly. And he bought himself shoes, and the right mantle, and put the right cloth over his head, hiding all the little scars. And the peasant said:

"Master, will you go forth from us?"

"Yea, for the time is come for me to return to men."

So he gave the peasant a piece of money, and said to him:

"Give me the cock that escaped and is now tied by the leg. For he shall go forth with me."

So for a piece of money the peasant gave the cock to the man who had died, and at dawn the man who had died set out into the phenomenal world, to be fulfilled in his own aloneness in the midst of it. For previously he had been too much identified with it. Then he had died. Now he must come back, to be alone in the midst. Yet even now he did not go quite alone, for under his arm, as he went, he carried the cock, whose tail fluttered gaily behind, and who craned his head excitedly, for he too was adventuring out for the first time into the wider phenomenal world, which is the stirring of the body of cocks also. And the peasant woman shed a few tears, but then went indoors, being a peasant, to look again at the pieces of money. And it seemed to her, a gleam came out of the pieces of money, wonderful.

The man who had died wandered on, and it was a sunny day. He looked around as he went, and stood aside as the pack-train passed by, towards the city. And he said to himself: Strange is the phenomenal world, dirty and clean together! And I am the same! Yet I am apart! And life bubbles everywhere, in me, in them, in this, in that. But it bubbles variously. Why should I ever have wanted it to bubble all alike? What a pity I preached to them! A sermon is so much more likely to cake into mud, and to close the fountains, than is a psalm or a song. I made a mistake. I understand that they executed me for preaching to them. Yet they could not finally execute me, for now I am risen in my own aloneness, and inherit the earth, since I lay no claim on it. And I will be alone in the seethe of all things; first and foremost, forever, I shall be alone. But I must toss this bird into the seethe of phenomena, for he must ride his wave. How hot he is with life! Soon, in some place, I shall leave him among the hens. And perhaps one evening I shall meet a woman who can lure my risen body, yet leave me my aloneness. For the body of my desire has died, and I am not in touch any more. Yet how do I know! All at least is life. And this cock gleams with bright aloneness, though he answers the lure of hens. And I shall hasten on to that village on the hill ahead of me; already I am tired and weak, and want to close my eyes to everything.

Hastening a little with the desire to have finished going, he overtook two men going slowly, and talking. And being soft-footed, he heard they were speaking of himself. And he remembered them, for he had known them in his life, the life of his mission. So he greeted them, but did not disclose himself in the dusk, and they did not know him. He said to them:

"What then of him who would be king, and was put to death for it?"

They answered suspiciously:

"Why ask you of him?"

"I have known him, and thought much about him," he said.

So they replied:

"He is risen."

"Yea! And where is he, and how does he live?"

"We know not, for it is not revealed. Yet he is risen, and in a little while will ascend unto the Father."

"Yea! And where then is his Father?"

"Know ye not? You are then of the gentiles! The Father is in heaven, above the cloud and the firmament."

"Truly? How then will he ascend?"

"As Elijah the prophet, he shall go up in a glory."

"Even into the sky?"

"Into the sky."

"Then he is not risen in the flesh?"

"He is risen in the flesh."

"And will he take flesh up into the sky?"

"The Father in heaven will take him up."

The man who had died said no more, for his say was over, and words beget words, even as gnats. But the men asked him:

"Why do you carry a cock?"

"I am a healer," he said, "and the bird hath virtue."

"You are not a believer?"

"Yea! I believe the bird is full of life and virtue."

They walked on in silence after this, and he felt they disliked his answer. So he was wary in himself, for a dangerous phenomenon in the world is a man of narrow belief, who denies the right of his neighbor to be alone. And as they came to the outskirts of the village, the man who had died stood still in the gloaming and said in his old voice:

"Know ye me not?"

And they cried in fear:

"Master!"

"Yea!" he said, mocking softly. And he turned suddenly away, down a side lane, and was gone under the wall before they knew.

So he came to an inn where the asses stood in the yard. And he called for fritters, and they were made for him. So he slept under a shed. But in the morning he was wakened by a loud crowing, and his cock's voice ringing in his ears. So he saw the rooster of the inn walking forth to battle, with his hens, a goodly number behind him. Then the cock of the man who had died sprang forth, and a battle began between the birds. The man of the inn ran to save his rooster, but the man who had died said:

"If my bird wins, I will give him thee. And if he lose, thou shalt eat him."

So the birds fought savagely, and the cock of the man who had died killed the common cock of the yard. Then the man who had died said to his young cock:

"Thou at least hast found thy kingdom, and the females to thy body. Thy aloneness can take on splendour, polished by the lure of thy hens."

And he left his bird there, and went on deeper into the phenomenal world, which is a vast complexity of entanglements and allurements. And he asked himself a last question: From what, and to what, could this infinite whirl be saved?

So he went his way, and was alone. But the way of the world was past belief, as he saw the strange entanglement of passions and circumstance and compulsion everywhere, but always the dread insomnia of compulsion. It was fear, the ultimate fear of death, that made men mad. So always he must move on, for if he stayed, his neighbours wound the strangling of their fear and bullying round him. There was nothing he could touch, for all, in a mad assertion of the ego, wanted to put a compulsion on him, and violate his intrinsic solitude. It was the mania of individuals, it was the mania of cities and societies and hosts, to lay a compulsion upon a man, upon all men. For men and women alike were mad with the egoistic fear of their own nothingness.

And he thought of his own mission, how he had tried to lay the compulsion of love on all men. And the old nausea came back on him. For there was no contact without a subtle attempt to inflict a compulsion. And already he had been compelled even into death. The nausea of the old wound broke out afresh, and he looked again on the world with repulsion, dreading its mean contacts.

PART II

The wind came cold and strong from inland, from the invisible snows of Lebanon. But the temple, facing south and west, towards Egypt, faced the splendid sun of winter as he curved down towards the sea, and warmth and radiance flooded in between the pillars of painted wood. But the sea was invisible, because of the trees, though its dashing sounded among the hum of pines. The air was turning golden to afternoon. The woman who served Isis stood in her yellow robe, and looked up at the steep slopes coming down to the sea, where the olive-trees silvered under the wind like water splashing. She was alone, save for the goddess. And in the winter afternoon the light stood erect and magnificent off the invisible sea, filling the hills of the coast. She went towards the sun, through the grove of Mediterranean pine-trees and evergreen oaks, in the midst of which the temple stood, on a little, tree-covered tongue of land between two bays.

It was only a very little way, and then she stood among the dry trunks of the outermost pines, on the rocks under which the sea smote and sucked, facing the open where the bright sun gloried in winter. The sea was dark, almost indigo, running away from the land, and crested with white. The hand of the wind brushed it strangely with shadow, as it brushed the olives of the slopes with silver. And there was no boat out.

The three boats were drawn high up on the steep shingle of the little bay, by the small grey tower. Along the edge of the shingle ran a high wall, inside which was a garden, occupying the brief flat of the bay, then rising in terraces up the steep slope of the coast. And there, some little way up, within another wall, stood the low white villa, white and alone on the coast, overlooking the sea. But higher, much higher up, where the olives had given way to pine-trees again, ran the coast road, keeping to the height to be above the gullies that came down to the bays.

Upon it all poured the royal sunshine of the January afternoon. Or rather, all was part of the great sun, glow and substance and immaculate loneliness of the sea, and pure brightness.

Crouching in the rocks above the dark water which only swung up and down, two slaves, half naked, were dressing pigeons for the evening meal. They pierced the throat of a blue, live bird, and let the drops of blood fall into the heaving sea, with curious concentration. They were performing some sacrifice, or working some incantation. The woman of the temple, yellow and white and alone like a winter narcissus, stood between the pines of the small, humped peninsula where the temple secretly hid, and watched.

A black-and-white pigeon, vividly white, like a ghost, suddenly escaped over the low dark sea, sped out, caught the wind, tilted, rose, soared and swept over the pine-trees, and wheeled away, a speck, inland. It had escaped. The priestess heard the cry of the boy slave, a garden slave of about seventeen. He raised his arms to heaven in anger as the pigeon wheeled away, naked and angry and young he held out his arms. Then he turned and seized the girl in an access of rage, and beat her with his fist that was stained with pigeon's blood. And she lay down with her face hidden, passive and quivering. The woman who owned them watched. And as she watched, she saw another onlooker, a stranger, in a low, broad hat, and a cloak of grey homespun, a dark-bearded man standing on the little causeway of rock that was the neck of her temple peninsula. By the blowing of his dark-grey cloak, she saw him. And he saw her, on the rocks like a white-and-yellow narcissus, because of the flutter of her white linen tunic, below the yellow mantle of wool. And both of them watched the two slaves.

The boy suddenly left off beating the girl. He crouched over her, touching her, trying to make her speak. But she lay quite inert, face down on the smoothed rock. And he put his arms round her and lifted her, but she slipped back to earth, like one dead, yet far too quick for anything dead. The boy, desperate, caught her by the hips and hugged her to him, turning her over there. There she seemed inert, all her fight was in her shoulders. He twisted her over, intent and unconscious, and pushed his hands between her thighs, to push them apart. And in an instant he was in to her, covering her in the blind, frightened frenzy of a boy's first coition. Quick and frenzied his young body quivered naked on hers, blind, for a minute. Then it lay quite still, as if dead.

And then, in terror, he peeped up. He peeped round, and drew slowly to his feet, adjusting his loin-rag. He saw the stranger, and then he saw, on the rocks beyond, the Lady of Isis, his mistress. And as he saw her, his whole body shrank and cowed, and with a strange, cringing motion he scuttled lamely towards the door in the wall.

The girl sat up and looked after him. When she had seen him disappear, she too looked round. And she saw the stranger and the priestess. Then with a sullen movement she turned away, as if she had seen nothing, to the four dead pigeons and the knife, which lay there on the rock. And she began to strip the small feathers, so that they rose on the wind like dust.

The priestess turned away. Slaves! Let the overseer watch them, she was not interested. She went slowly through the pines again, back to the temple, which stood in the sun in a small clearing, at the centre of the tongue of land. It was a small temple of wood, painted all pink and white and blue, having at the front four wooden pillars rising like stems to the swollen lotus-bud of Egypt at the top, supporting the roof and the open, spiky lotus-flowers of the outer frieze, which went round under the eaves. Two low steps of stone led up to the platform before the pillars, and the chamber behind the pillars was open. There a low stone altar stood, with a few embers in its hollow, and the dark stain of blood in its end groove.

She knew her temple so well, for she had built it at her own expense, and tended it for seven years. There it stood, pink and white like a flower in the little clearing, backed by blackish evergreen oaks; and the shadow of afternoon was already washing over its pillar-bases.

She entered slowly, passing through to the dark inner chamber, lighted by a perfumed oil-flame. And once more she pushed shut the door, and once more she threw a few grains of incense on the brazier before the goddess, and once more she sat down before her goddess, in the almost-darkness, to muse, to go away into the dream of the goddess.

It was Isis, but not Isis, Mother of Horus. It was Isis Bereaved, Isis in Search. The goddess in painted marble lifted her face, and strode, one thigh forward, through the frail fluting of her robe, in the anguish of bereavement and of search. She was looking for the fragments of the dead Osiris, dead and scattered asunder, dead, torn apart, and thrown in fragments over the wide world. And she must find his hands and his feet, his heart, his thighs, his head, his belly, she must gather him together and fold her arms round the re-assembled body till it became warm again, and roused to life, and could embrace her and fecundate her womb. And the strange rapture and anguish of search went on through the years, as she lifted her throat, and her hollowed eyes looked inward, in the tormented ecstasy of seeking, and the delicate navel of her bud-like belly showed through the frail, girdled robe with the eternal asking, asking, of her search. And through the years she found him bit by bit, heart and head and limbs and body. And yet she had not found the last reality, the final clue to him, the genitals that alone could bring him really back to her, and touch her womb. For she was Isis of the subtle lotus, the womb which waits submerged and in bud, waits for the touch of that other, inward sun that streams its rays from the loins of the male Osiris.

This was the mystery the woman had served alone for seven years, since she was twenty, till now she was twenty-seven. Before, when she was young, she had lived in the world, in Rome, in Ephesus, in Egypt. For her father had been one of Anthony's captains and comrades, had fought with Anthony and had stood with him when Caesar was murdered, and through to the days of shame. Then he had come again across to Asia, out of favour with Rome, and had been killed in the mountains beyond Lebanon. The widow, having no favour to hope for from Octavius, had retired to her small property on the coast under Lebanon, taking her daughter from the world, a girl of nineteen, beautiful but unmarried.

When she was young the girl had known Caesar, and had shrunk from his eagle-like rapacity. The golden Anthony had sat with her many a half-hour, in the splendour of his great limbs and glowing manhood, and talked with her of the philosophies and the gods. For he was fascinated as a child by the gods, though he mocked at them, and forgot them in his own vanity.—But he said to her: I have sacrified two doves for you, to Venus, for I am afraid you make no offering to the sweet goddess. Beware, you will offend her. Come, why is the flower of you so cool within? Does never a ray nor a glance find its way through? Ah come, a maid should open her bud to the sun, when the sun leans towards her to caress her.—And the big, bright eyes of Anthony laughed down on her, bathing her in his glow. And she felt the lovely glow of his male beauty and his amorousness bathe all her limbs and her body. But it was as he said: the very flower of her womb was cool, was almost cold, like a bud in shadow of frost, for all the flooding of his sunshine. So Anthony, respecting her father, who loved her, had left her.

And it had always been the same. She saw many men, young and old. And on the whole, she liked the old ones best, for they talked to her still and sincere, and did not expect her to open like a flower to the sun of their maleness. Once she asked a philosopher: Are all women born to be given to men?—To which the old man answered slowly: Rare women wait for the re-born man. For the lotus, as you know, will not answer to all the bright heat of the sun. But she curves her dark, hidden head in the depths, and stirs not. Till, in the night, one of those rare invisible suns that have been killed and shine no more, rises among the stars in unseen purple, and like the violet, sends its rare, purple rays out into the night. To these the lotus stirs as to a caress, and rises upwards through the flood, and lifts up her bent head, and opens with an expansion such as no other flower knows, and spreads her sharp rays of bliss, and offers her soft, gold depth such as no other flower possesses, to the penetration of the flooding, violet-dark sun that has died and risen and makes no show. But for the golden brief-day suns of show, such as Anthony, and for the hard winter suns of power, such as Caesar, the lotus stirs not, nor will ever stir. Those will only tear open the bud. Ah, I tell you, wait for the re-born, and wait for the bud to stir.

So she had waited, but the bud of her womb had never stirred. For all the men were soldiers or politicians in the Roman spell, assertive, manly, splendid apparently, but of an inward meanness, an inadequacy. And never once had her womb stirred its lotus bud, though the maleness of men had caressed the surface of her being like a pool. And Rome and Egypt alike had left her alone, unroused. And she was a woman to herself, she would not give herself for a surface glow, nor marry for reasons. She would wait for the lotus to stir.

And then, in Egypt, she had found Isis, in whom she spelled her mystery. So she brought Isis to the shores of Sidon, and lived with her in the mystery of search; whilst her mother, who loved affairs, controlled the small estate and the slaves, with a free hand.

When the woman had roused from her muse and risen to perform the last brief ritual to Isis, she replenished the lamp and left the sanctuary, locking the door. In the outer world, the sun had already set, and twilight was chill among the humming trees, which hummed still, though the wind was abating.

A stranger in a dark, broad hat rose from the corner of the temple steps, holding his hat in the wind. He was dark-faced, with a black pointed beard.

"O Madam, whose shelter may I implore?" he said to the woman who stood in her yellow mantle on the step above him, beside a pink-and-white painted pillar. Her face was rather long and pale, her dusky-blond hair was held under a thin gold net. She looked down on the vagabond with indifference. It was the same she had seen watching the slaves.

"Why come you down from the road?" she asked.

"I saw the temple like a pale flower on the coast, and would rest among the trees of the precincts, if the Lady of the goddess permits."

"It is Isis in Search," she said, answering his first question.

"The goddess is great," he replied.

She looked at him still with mistrust. There was a faint, remote smile in the dark eyes lifted to her, though the face was hollow with suffering. The vagabond divined her hesitation, and was mocking her.

"Stay here upon the steps," she said. "A slave shall show you the shelter."

"The Lady of Egypt is gracious."

She went down the rocky path of the humped peninsula, in her gilded sandals. Beautiful were her ivory feet, beneath the white tunic, and above the saffron mantle her dusky-blond head bent as with endless musings. A woman entangled in her own dream. The man smiled a little, half-bitterly, and sat again on the step to wait, drawing his mantle round him, in the cold twilight.

At length a slave appeared, also in hodden grey.

"Seek ye the shelter of our Lady?" he said insolently.

"Even so."

"Then come."

With the brusque insolence of a slave waiting on a vagabond, the young fellow led through the trees and down into a little gully in the rock, where, almost in darkness, was a small cave, with a litter of the tall heaths that grew on the waste places of the coast, under the stone-pines. The place was dark, but absolutely silent from the wind. There was still a faint odour of goats.

"Here sleep!" said the slave. "For the goats come no more on this half-island. And there is water!" He pointed to a little basin of rock where the maidenhair fern fringed a dripping mouthful of water.

Having scornfully bestowed his patronage, the slave departed. The man who had died climbed out to the tip of the peninsula, where the waves thrashed. It was rapidly getting dark, and the stars were coming out. The wind was abating for the night. In-land, the steep grooved upslope was dark, to the long wavering outline of the crest against the translucent sky. Only now and then a lantern flickered towards the villa.

The man who had died went back to the shelter. There he took bread from his leather pouch, dipped it in the water of the tiny spring, and slowly ate. Having eaten and washed his mouth, he looked once more at the bright stars in the pure, windy sky, then settled the heath for his bed. Having laid his hat and his sandals aside, and put his pouch under his cheek for a pillow, he slept, for he was very tired. Yet during the night the cold woke him, pinching wearily through his weariness. Outside was brilliantly starry, and still windy. He sat and hugged himself in a sort of coma, and towards dawn went to sleep again.

In the morning, the coast was still chill in shadow, though the sun was up behind the hills, when the woman came down from the villa towards the goddess. The sea was fair and pale-blue, lovely in newness, and at last the wind was still. Yet the waves broke white in the many rocks, and tore in the shingle of the little bay. The woman came slowly, towards her dream. Yet she was aware of an interruption.

As she followed the little neck of rock on to her peninsula, and climbed the slope between the trees to the temple, a slave came down and stood, making his obeisance. There was a faint insolence in his humility.

"Speak!" she said.

"Lady, the man is there, he still sleeps. Lady, may I speak?"

"Speak!" she said, repelled by the fellow.

"Lady, the man is an escaped malefactor." The slave seemed to triumph in imparting this unpleasant news.

"By what sign?"

"Behold, his hands and feet! Will the Lady look on him?"

"Lead on!"

The slave led quickly over the mound of the hill down to the tiny ravine. There he stood aside, and the woman went into the crack towards the cave. Her heart beat a little. Above all, she must preserve her temple inviolate.

The vagabond was asleep with his cheek on his scrip, his mantle wrapped round him, but his bare, soiled feet curling side by side, to keep each other warm, and his hand lying loosely clenched in sleep. And in the pale skin of the feet, usually covered by sandal-straps, she saw the scars, and in the palm of the loose hand.

She had no interest in men, particularly in the servile class. Yet she looked at the sleeping face. It was worn, hollow, and rather ugly. But, a true priestess, she saw the other kind of beauty in it, the sheer stillness of the deeper life. There was even a sort of majesty in the dark brows, over the still, hollow cheeks. She saw that his black hair, left long, in contrast to the Roman fashion, was touched with grey at the temples, and the black pointed beard had threads of grey. But that must be suffering or misfortune, for the man was young. His dusky skin had the silvery glisten of youth still.

There was a beauty of much suffering, and the strange calm candour of finer life in the whole delicate ugliness of the face. For the first time, she was touched on the quick at the sight of a man, as if the tip of a fine flame of living had touched her. It was the first time. Men had roused all kinds of feelings in her, but never had touched her on the yearning quick of her womb, with the flame-tip of life.

She went back under the rock to where the slave waited.

"Know!" she said. "This is no malefactor, but a free citizen of the east. Do not disturb him. But when he comes forth, bring him to me, tell him I would speak with him."

She spoke coldly, for she found slaves invariably repellent, a little repulsive. They were so imbedded in the lesser life, and their appetites and their small consciousness were a little disgusting. So she wrapped her dream round her, and went to the temple, where a slave-girl brought winter roses and jasmine, for the altar. But to-day, even in her ministrations, she was disturbed.

The sun rose over the hill, sparkling, the light fell triumphantly on the little pine-covered peninsula of the coast, and on the pink temple, in pristine newness. The man who had died woke up, and put on his sandals. He put on his hat too, slung his scrip under his mantle, and went out, to see the morning in all its blue and its new gold. He glanced at the little yellow-and-white narcissus sparkling gaily in the rocks. And he saw the slave waiting for him, like a menace.

"Master," said the slave. "Our Lady would speak with you at the house of Isis."

"It is well," said the wanderer.

He went slowly, staying to look at the pale-blue sea, like a flower in unruffled bloom, and the white fringes among the rocks, like white rock-flowers, the hollow slopes sheering up high from the shore, grey with olive-trees and green with bright young wheat, and set with the white small villa. All fair and pure in the January morning.

The sun fell on the corner of the temple, he sat down on the step, in the sunshine, in the infinte patience of waiting. He had come back to life, but not to the same life that he had left, the life of little people and the little day. Re-born, he was in the other life, the greater day of the human consciousness. And he was alone and apart from the little day, and out of contact with the daily people. Not yet had he accepted the irrevocable *noli me tangere* which separates the re-born from the vulgar. The separation was absolute, and yet here at the temple he felt peace, the hard, bright pagan peace with hostilty of slaves beneath.

The woman came into the dark inner doorway of the temple, from the shrine, and stood there hesitating. She could see the dark figure of the man sitting on the steps by the pink-and-blue pillar, sitting in that terrible stillness that was portentous to her, had something almost menacing in its patience.

She advanced across the outer chamber of the temple, and the man, becoming aware of her, stood up. She addressed him in Greek, but he said:

"Madam, my Greek is limited. Allow me to speak vulgar Syrian."

"Whence come you? Whither go you?" she asked, with the hurried preoccupation of a priestess.

"From the east beyond Damascus—and I go west as the road goes," he replied, slowly.

She glanced at him with sudden anxiety and shyness.

"But why do you have the marks of a malefactor?" she asked abruptly.

"Did the Lady of Isis spy upon me in my sleep?" he asked, with a grey weariness.

"The slave warned me—Your hands and feet—" she said.

He looked at her. Then he said:

"Will the Lady of Isis allow me to bid her farewell, and go up to the road?"

The wind came in a sudden puff, lifting his mantle and his hat. He put up his hand to hold the brim, and she saw again the thin brown hand with its scar.

"See! the scar!" she said, pointing.

"Even so!" he said. "But farewell, and to Isis my homage and my thanks for sleep."

He was going. But she looked at him with her wondering blue eyes.

"Will you not look on Isis?" she said, with sudden impulse. And something stirred in him, like pain.

"Where then?" he said.

"Come!"

He followed her into the inner shrine, into the almost darkness. When his eyes got used to the faint glow of the lamp, he saw the goddess striding like a ship, eager in the swirl of her gown, and he made his obeisance.

"Great is Isis!" he said. "In her search she is greater than death. Wonderful is such walking in a woman, wonderful the goal. All men praise thee, Isis, thou greater than the mother unto man."

The woman of Isis heard, and threw incense on the brazier. Then she looked at the man.

"Is it well with thee here?" she asked him. "Has Isis brought thee home to herself?"

He looked at the priestess in wonder and trouble.

"I know not," he said.

But the woman was pondering, that this was the lost Osiris. She felt it in the quick of her soul. And her agitation was intense.

He could not stay in the close, dark, perfumed shrine. He went

45

out again to the morning, to the cold air. He felt something approaching to touch him, and all his flesh was still woven with pain and the wild commandment: *Noli me tangere!* Touch me not! Oh, don't touch me!

The woman followed into the open with timid eagerness. He was moving away.

"O stranger, do not go! O stay awhile with Isis!"

He looked at her, at her face open like a flower, as if a sun had risen in her soul. And again his loins stirred.

"Would you detain me, girl of Isis?" he said.

"Stay! I am sure you are Osiris!" she said.

He laughed suddenly.

"Not yet!" he said. Then he looked at her wistful face. "But I will sleep another night in the cave of the goats, if Isis wills it," he added.

She put her hands together with a priestess' childish happiness.

"Ah, Isis will be glad!" she said.

So he went down to the shore, in great trouble, saying to himself: Shall I give myself into this touch? Shall I give myself into this touch? Men have tortured me to death with their touch. Yet this girl of Isis is a tender flame of healing. I am a physician, yet I have no healing like the flame of this tender girl. The flame of this tender girl! Like the first pale crocus of the spring. How could I have been blind to the healing and the bliss in the crocus-like body of a tender woman! Ah tenderness! more terrible and lovely than the death I died—

He prised small shell-fish from the rocks, and ate them with relish and wonder for the simple taste of the sea. And inwardly he was tremulous, thinking: Dare I come into touch? For this is further than death. I have dared let them lay hands on me and put me to death. But dare I come into this tender touch of life? Oh this is harder—

But the woman went into the shrine again, and sat rapt in pure muse, through the long hours, watching the swirling stride of the yearning goddess, and the navel of the bud-like belly, like a seal on the virgin urge of the search. And she gave herself to the woman-flow and to the urge of Isis in Search.

Towards sundown she went on the peninsula to look for him. And she found him gone towards the sun, as she had gone the day before, and sitting on the pine-needles at the foot of the tree, where she had stood when first she saw him. Now she approached tremulously and slowly, afraid lest he did not want her. She stood near him unseen, till suddenly he glanced up at her from under his broad hat, and saw the westering sun on her netted hair. He was startled, yet he expected her.

"Is that your home?" he said, pointing to the white low villa on the slope of olives.

"It is my mother's house. She is a widow, and I am her only child."

"And are these all her slaves?"

"Except those that are mine."

Their eyes met for a moment.

"Will you too sit to see the sun go down?" he said.

He had not risen to speak to her. He had known too much pain. So she sat on the dry brown pine-needles, gathering her saffron mantle round her knees. A boat was coming in, out of the open glow into the shadow of the bay, and slaves were lifting the small nets, their babble coming off the surface of the water.

"And this is home to you," he said.

"But I serve Isis in Search," she replied.

He looked at her. She was like a soft, musing cloud, somehow remote. His soul smote him with passion and compassion.

"Mayst thou find thy desire, Maiden," he said, with sudden earnestness.

"And art thou not Osiris?" she asked.

He flushed suddenly.

"Yea, if thou wilt heal me!" he said. "For the death-aloofness is still upon me, and I cannot escape it."

She looked at him for a moment in fear from the soft, blue suns of her eyes. Then she lowered her head, and they sat in silence in the warmth and glow of the great western sun: the man who had died, and the woman of the pure search.

The sun was curving down to the sea, in grand winter splendour. It fell on the twinkling, naked bodies of the slaves, with their ruddy broad hams and their small black heads, as they ran spreading the nets on the pebble beach. The all-tolerant Pan watched over them. All-tolerant Pan should be their god forever.

The woman rose as the sun's rim dipped, saying:

"If you will stay, I shall send down victual and covering."

"The lady your mother, what will she say?"

The woman of Isis looked at him strangely, but with a tinge of misgiving.

"It is my own," she said.

"It is good," he said, smiling faintly, and foreseeing difficulties.

He watched her go, with her absorbed, strange motion of the self-dedicate. Her dun head was a little bent, the white linen swung about her ivory ankles. And he saw the naked slaves stand to look at her, with a certain wonder, and even a certain mischief. But she passed intent through the door in the wall, on the bay.

But the man who had died sat on at the foot of the tree overlooking the strand, for on the little shore everything happened. At the small stream which ran in round the corner of the property wall, women slaves were still washing linen, and now and again came the hollow chock! chock! chock! as they beat it against the smooth stones, in the dark little hollow of the pool. There was a smell of olive-refuse on the air; and sometimes still the faint rumble of the grindstone that was milling the olives, inside the garden, and the sound of the slave calling to the ass at the mill. Then through the doorway a woman stepped, a grey-haired woman in a mantle of whitish wool, and there followed her a bare-headed man in a toga, a Roman: probably her steward or overseer. They stood on the high shingle above the sea, and cast round a rapid glance. The broad-hammed, ruddy-bodied slaves bent absorbed and abject over the nets, picking them clean, the women washing linen thrust their palms with energy down on the wash, the old slave bent absorbed at the water's edge, washing the fish and the polyps of the catch. And the woman and the overseer saw it all, in one glance. They also saw, seated at the foot of the tree on the rocks of the peninsula, the strange man silent and alone. And the man who had died saw that they spoke of him. Out of the little sacred world of the peninsula he looked on the common world, and saw it still hostile.

The sun was touching the sea, across the tiny bay stretched the shadow of the opposite humped headland. Over the shingle, now blue and cold in shadow, the elderly woman trod heavily, in shadow too, to look at the fish spread in the flat basket of the old man crouching at the water's edge; a naked old slave with fat hips and shoulders, on whose soft, fairish-orange body the last sun twinkled, then died. The old slave continued cleaning the fish absorbedly, not looking up: as if the lady were the shadow of twilight falling on him.

Then from the gateway stepped two slave-girls with flat baskets on their heads, and from one basket the terra-cotta wine-jar and the oil-jar poked up, leaning slightly. Over the massive shingle, under the wall, came the girls, and the woman of Isis in her saffron mantle stepped in twilight after them. Out at sea the sun still shone. Here was shadow.

The mother with grey head stood at the sea's edge and watched the daughter, all yellow and white, with dun blond head, swinging unseeing and unheeding after the slave-girls, towards the neck of rock of the peninsula: the daughter, travelling in her absorbed other-world. And not moving from her place, the elderly mother watched that procession of three file up the rise of the headland, between the trees, and disappear, shut in by trees. No slave had lifted a head to look. The grey-haired woman still watched the trees where her daughter had disappeared. Then she glanced again at the foot of the tree, where the man who had died still was sitting, inconspicuous now, for the sun had left him; and only the far blade of the sea shone bright. It was evening. Patience! Let destiny move!

The mother plodded with a stamping stride up the shingle: not long and swinging and rapt, like the daughter, but short and determined. Then down the rocks opposite came two naked slaves trotting with huge bundles of dark green on their shoulders, so their broad, naked legs twinkled underneath like insects' legs, and their

49

heads were hidden. They came trotting across the shingle, heedless and intent on their way, when suddenly the man, the Roman-looking overseer, addressed them, and they stopped dead. They stood invisible under their loads, as if they might disappear altogether, now they were arrested. Then a hand came out and pointed to the peninsula. Then the two green-heaped slaves trotted on, towards the temple precincts. The grey-haired woman joined the man, and slowly the two passed through the door again, from the shingle of the sea to the property of the villa. Then the old, fat-shouldered slave rose, pallid in shadow, with his tray of fish from the sea, and the women rose from the pool, dusky and alive, piling the wet linen in a heap on to the flat baskets, and the slaves who had cleaned the net gathered its whitish folds together. And the old slave with the fish-basket on his shoulder, and the women-slaves with heaped baskets of wet linen on their heads, and the two slaves with the folded net, and the slave with oars on his shoulders, and the boy with the folded sail on his arm, gathered in a naked group near the door, and the man who had died heard the low buzz of their chatter. Then as the wind wafted cold, they began to pass through the door.

It was the life of the little day, the life of little people. And the man who had died said to himself: Unless we encompass it in the greater day, and set the little life in the circle of the greater life, all is disaster.

Even the tops of the hills were in shadow. Only the sky was still upwardly radiant. The sea was a vast milky shadow. The man who had died rose a little stiffly, and turned into the grove.

There was no one at the temple. He went on to his lair in the rock. There, the slave-men had carried out the old heath of the bedding, swept the rock floor, and were spreading with nice art the myrtle, then the rougher heath, then the soft, bushy heath-tips on top, for a bed. Over it all they put a well-tanned white ox-skin. The maids had laid folded woollen covers at the head of the cave, and the wine-jar, the oil-jar, a terra-cotta drinking-cup, and a basket containing bread, salt, cheese, dried figs and eggs stood neatly arranged. There was also a little brazier of charcoal. The cave was suddenly full, and a dwelling-place.

The woman of Isis stood in the hollow by the tiny spring. Only one slave at a time could pass. The girl-slaves waited at the entrance to the narrow place. When the man who had died appeared, the woman sent the girls away. The men-slaves still arranged the bed, making the job as long as possible. But the woman of Isis dismissed them too. And the man who had died came to look at his house.

"Is it well?" the woman asked him.

"It is very well," the man replied. "But the lady your mother, and he who is no doubt the steward, watched while the slaves brought the goods. Will they not oppose you?"

"I have my own portion! Can I not give of my own? Who is going to oppose me and the gods?" she said, with a certain soft fury, touched with exasperation. So that he knew her mother would oppose her, and that the spirit of the little life would fight against the spirit of the greater. And he thought: Why did the woman of Isis relinquish her portion in the daily world? She should have kept her goods fiercely!

"Will you eat and drink?" she said. "On the ashes are warm eggs. And I will go up to the meal at the villa. But in the second hour of the night I shall come down to the temple. Oh, then, will you too come to Isis?" She looked at him, and a queer glow dilated her eyes. This was her dream, and it was greater than herself. He could not bear to thwart her or hurt her in the least thing now. She was in the full glow of her woman's mystery.

"Shall I wait at the temple?" he said.

"Oh, wait in the second hour, and I shall come." He heard the humming supplication in her voice, and his fibres quivered.

"But the lady, your mother—?" he said gently.

The woman looked at him, startled.

"She will not thwart me!" she said.

So he knew that the mother would thwart the daughter, for the daughter had left her goods in the hands of her mother, who would hold fast to this power.

But she went, and the man who had died lay reclining on his couch, and ate the eggs from the ashes, and dipped his bread in oil, and ate it, for his flesh was dry: and he mixed wine and water, and drank. And so he lay still, and the lamp made a small bud of light.

He was absorbed and enmeshed in new sensations. The woman of Isis was lovely to him, not so much in form, as in the wonderful womanly glow of her. Suns beyond suns had dipped her in mysterious fire, the mysterious fire of a potent woman, and to touch her was like touching the sun. Best of all was her tender desire for him, like sunshine, so soft and still. She is like sunshine upon me, he said to himself, stretching his limbs. I have never before stretched my limbs in such sunshine, as her desire for me. The greatest of all gods granted me this.

At the same time, he was haunted by fear of the outer world. If they can, they will kill us, he said to himself. But there is a law of the sun which protects us.

And he said again to himself: I have risen naked and branded. But if I am naked enough for this contact, I have not died in vain. Before I was clogged.

He rose and went out. The night was chill and starry, and of a great wintry splendour. "There are destinies of splendour," he said to the night, "after all our doom of littleness and meanness and pain."

So he went up silently to the temple, and waited in darkness against the inner wall, looking out on grey darkness, stars, and rims of trees. And he said again to himself: There are destinies of splendour, and there is a greater power.

So at last he saw the light of her silk lanthorn swinging, coming intermittent between the trees, yet coming swiftly. She was alone, and near, the light softly swishing on her mantle-hem. And he trembled with fear and with joy, saying to himself: I am almost more afraid of this touch than I was of death. For I am more nakedly exposed to it.

"I am here, Lady of Isis," he said softly out of the dark.

"Ah!" she cried, in fear also, yet in rapture. For she was given to her dream.

She unlocked the door of the shrine, and he followed after her.

Then she latched the door shut again. The air inside was warm and close and perfumed. The man who had died stood by the closed door and watched the woman. She had come first to the goddess. And dim-lit the goddess statue stood surging forward, a little fearsome, like a great woman-presence urging.

The priestess did not look at him. She took off her saffron mantle and laid it on a low couch. In the dim light she was bare-armed, in her girdled white tunic. But she was still hiding herself away from him. He stood back in shadow, and watched her softly fan the brazier and fling on incense. Faint clouds of sweet aroma arose on the air. She turned to the statue in the ritual of approach, softly swaying forward with a slight lurch, like a moored boat, tipping towards the goddess.

He watched the strange rapt woman, and he said to himself: I must leave her alone in her rapture, her female mysteries. So she tipped in her strange forward-swaying rhythm before the goddess. Then she broke into a murmur of Greek, which he could not understand. And as she murmured her swaying softly subsided, like a boat on a sea that grows still. And as he watched her, he saw her soul in its aloneness, and its female difference. He said to himself: How different she is from me, how strangely different! She is afraid of me, and my male difference. She is getting herself naked and clear of her fear. How sensitive and softly alive she is! How alive she is, with a life so different from mine! How beautiful, with a soft, strange courage of life, so different from my courage of death! What a beautiful thing, like the heart of a rose, like the core of a flame. She is making herself completely penetrable. Ah, how terrible to fail her, or to trespass on her!

She turned to him, her face glowing from the goddess.

"You are Osiris, aren't you?" she said naively.

"If you will," he said.

"Will you let Isis discover you? Will you take off your things, and come to Isis?"

He looked at the woman, and lost his breath. And his wounds, and especially the death-wound through his belly, began to cry again.

"It has hurt so much!" he said. "You must forgive me if I am still held back."

But he took off his cloak and his tunic, and went naked towards the idol, his breast panting with the sudden terror of overwhelming pain, memory of overwhelming pain, and grief too bitter.

"They did me to death!" he said in excuse of himself, turning his face to her for a moment. And she saw the ghost of the death in him, as he stood there thin and stark before her, and suddenly she was terrified, and she felt robbed. She felt the shadow of the grey, grisly wing of death triumphant.

"Ah Goddess," he said to the idol, in the vernacular. "I would be so glad to live, if you would give me my clue again."

For here again he felt desperate, faced by the demand of life, and burdened still by his death.

"Let me anoint you!" the woman said to him softly. "Let me anoint the scars! Show me, and let me anoint them!"

He forgot his nakedness in this re-evoked old pain. He sat on the edge of the couch, and she poured a little ointment into the palm of his hand. And as she chafed his hand, it all came back, the nails, the holes, the cruelty, the unjust cruelty against him who had offered only kindness. The agony of injustice and cruelty came over him again, as in his death-hour. But she chafed the palm, murmuring:

"What was torn becomes a new flesh, what was a wound is full of fresh life, this scar is the eye of the violet."

And he could not help smiling at her, in her naïf priestess' absorption. This was her dream, and he was only a dream-object to her. She would never know or understand what he was. Especially she would never know the death that was gone before in him. But what did it matter? She was different. She was woman: her life and her death were different from his. Only she was good to him.

When she chafed his feet with oil and tender healing, he could not refrain from saying to her:

"Once a woman washed my feet with tears, and wiped them with her hair, and poured on precious ointment."

The woman of Isis looked up at him from her earnest work, interrupted again.

"Were they hurt then?" she said. "Your feet?"

"No no! It was while they were whole."

"And did you love her?"

"Love had passed in her. She only wanted to serve," he replied. "She had been a prostitute."

"And did you let her serve you?" she asked.

"Yea."

"Did you let her serve you with the corpse of her love?"

"Ay!"

Suddenly it dawned on him: I asked them all to serve me with the corpse of their love. And in the end I offered them only the corpse of my love. This is my body—take and eat—my corpse—

A vivid shame went through him.—After all, he thought,—I wanted them to love with dead bodies. If I had kissed Judas with live love, perhaps he would never have kissed me with death. Perhaps he loved me in the flesh, and I willed that he should love me bodilessly, with the corpse of love—

There dawned on him the reality of the soft warm love which is in touch, and which is full of delight.—And I told them, blessed are they that mourn, he said to himself.—Alas, if I mourned even this woman here, now I am in death, I should have to remain dead. And I want so much to live. Life has brought me to this woman with warm hands. And her touch is more to me now than all my words. For I want to live—

"Go then to the Goddess!" she said softly, gently pushing him towards Isis. And as he stood there dazed and naked as an unborn thing, he heard the woman murmuring to the goddess, murmuring, murmuring with a plaintive appeal. She was stooping now, looking at the scar in the soft flesh of the socket of his side, a scar deep and like an eye sore with endless weeping, just in the soft socket above the hip. It was here that his blood had left him, and his water, and his essential seed. The woman was trembling softly and murmuring in Greek. And he, in the recurring dismay of having died, and in the anguished perplexity of having tried to force life, felt his wounds crying aloud, and his bowels and the deep places of his body howling again: I have been murdered, and I lent myself to murder. They murdered me, but I lent myself to murder—

The woman, silent now, but quivering, laid oil in her hand and put her palm over the wound in his right side. He winced, and the wound absorbed his life again, as thousands of times before. And in the dark, wild pain and panic of his consciousness rang only one cry: Oh, how can she take this death out of me? How can she take from me this death? She can never know! She can never understand! She can never equal it . . . !

In silence, she softly, rhythmically chafed the scar with oil, absorbed now in her priestess' task, softly, softly gathering power, while the vitals of the man howled in panic. But as she gradually gathered power, and passed in a girdle round him to the opposite scar, gradually warmth began to take the place of the cold terror, and he felt: I am going to be flushed warm again, I am going to be whole! I shall be warm like the morning. I shall be a man. It doesn't need understanding. It needs newness. She brings me newness—

And he listened to the faint, ceaseless wail of distress of his wounds, sounding as if for ever under the horizons of his consciousness. But the wail was growing dim, more dim.

He thought of the woman toiling over him: She does not know! She does not realise the death in me. But she has another consciousness. She comes to me from the opposite end of the night.

Having chafed all his lower body with oil, his belly, his buttocks, even the slain penis and the sad stones, having worked with her slow intensity of a priestess, so that the sound of his wounds grew dimmer and dimmer, suddenly she put her breast against the wound in his left side, and her arms round him, folding over the wound in his right side, and she pressed him to her, in a power of living warmth, like in the folds of a river. And the wailing died out altogether, and there was stillness and darkness in his soul, unbroken dark stillness, wholeness.

Then slowly, slowly, in the perfect darkness of his inner man, he felt the stir of something coming: a dawn, a new sun. A new sun was coming up in him, in the perfect inner darkness of himself. He waited for it breathless, quivering with fearful hope.

"Now I am not myself—I am something new—"

And as it rose, he felt, with a cold breath of disappointment, the girdle of the living woman slip from him, the warmth and the glow slipped down from him, leaving him stark. She crouched spent at the feet of the goddess, hiding her face.

He quivered, as the sun burst up in his body. Stooping, he laid his hand softly on her warm, bright shoulder, and the shock of desire went through him, shock after shock, so that he wondered if it were another sort of death. But full of magnificence.

Now all his consciousness was there in the crouching, hidden woman. He stooped beside her and caressed her softly, blindly, murmuring inarticulate things. And his death and his passion of sacrifice were all as nothing to him now, he knew only the crouching fulness of the woman there, the soft white rock of life.

"On this rock I build my life!"

The deep-folded, penetrable rock of the living woman! the woman, hiding her face. Himself bending over, powerful and new like dawn. He crouched to her, and he felt the blaze of his manhood and his power rise up in his loins, magnificent.

"I am risen!"

Magnificent, blazing indomitable in the depths of his loins, his own sun dawned, and sent its fire running along his limbs, so that his face shone unconsciously.

He untied the string of the linen tunic, and slipped the garment down, till he saw the white glow of her white-gold breasts. And he touched them, and he felt his life go molten.—Father! he said—Why did you hide this from me?—And he touched her with the poignancy of wonder, and the marvellous piercing transcendence of desire.—Lo! he said.—This is beyond prayer.—It was the deep, interfolded warmth, warmth living and penetrable, the woman, the heart of the rose! —My mansion is the intricate warm rose, my joy is this blossom!

She looked up at him suddenly, her face like a lifted light, wistful, tender, her eyes like many wet flowers. And he drew her to his breast with a passion of tenderness and consuming desire, and a last thought: My hour is upon me, I am taken unawares—

So he knew her, and was at one with her.

Afterwards, with a dim wonder, she touched the great scars in his sides with her finger-tips, and said:

"But they no longer hurt?"

"They are suns!" he said. "They shine from your touch. They are my atonement with you."

And his desire flamed sunwise again, towards her, so he knew her again, and his bowels gloried in her. And as they lay in stillness, belly to belly, her bowels praised life.

When they left the temple, it was the coldness before dawn. As he closed the door, he looked again at the goddess, and he said:

"Lo, Isis is a kindly goddess, and full of tenderness. Great gods are warm-hearted and have tender goddesses."

The woman wrapped herself in her mantle and went home in silence, sightless, brooding like the lotus softly shutting again, with its gold core full of fresh life. She saw nothing, for her own petals were a sheath to her. Only she thought: I am full of Osiris. I am full of the risen Osiris!

But the man looked at the vivid stars before dawn, as they rained down to the sea, and the dog-star green towards the sea's rim. And he thought: How plastic it is, how full of curves and folds like an invisible rose of dark-petalled openness, that shows where dew touches its darkness! How full it is, and great beyond all gods. How it leans around me, and I am part of it, the great rose of space. I am like a grain of its perfume, and the woman is a grain of its beauty. Now the world is one flower of many-petalled darknesses, and I am in its perfume as in a touch.

So, in the absolute stillness and fulness of touch, he slept in his cave while the dawn came. And after the dawn, the wind rose and brought a storm, with cold rain. So he stayed in his cave in the peace and the delight of being in touch, delighting to hear the sea, and the rain on the earth, and to see one white-and-gold narcissus bowing wet, and still wet. And he said: This is the great atonement, the being in touch. The grey sea and the rain, the wet narcissus and the woman I wait for, the invisible Isis and the unseen sun are all in touch, and at one.

He waited at the temple for the woman, and she came in the rain. But she said to him:

"Let me sit still awhile with Isis. And come to me, will you come to me, in the second hour of night?"

So he went back to the cave and lay in stillness and in the joy of being in touch, waiting for the woman who would come with the night, and consummate again the contact. Then when night came the woman came, and came gladly, for her great yearning too was upon her, to be in touch, to be in touch with him, nearer.

So the days came, and the nights came, and the days came again, and the contact was perfected and fulfilled. And he said: I will ask her nothing, not even her name, for a name would set her apart. And she said to herself: He is Osiris. I wish to know no more.

Plum-blossom blew from the trees, the time of the narcissus was past, anemones lit up the ground and were gone, the perfume of bean-fields was in the air. All changed, the blossom of the universe changed its petals and swung round to look another way. The spring was fulfilled, a contact was established, the man and the woman were fulfilled of one another, and departure was in the air.

One day he met her under the trees, when the morning sun was hot, and the pines smelled sweet, and on the hills the last pear-bloom was scattering. She came slowly towards him, and in her gentle lingering, her tender hanging back from him, he knew a change in her.

"Hast thou conceived?" he asked her.

"Why?" she said.

"Thou art like a tree whose green leaves follow the blossoms, full of sap. And there is a withdrawing about thee."

"It is so," she said. "I am with young by thee. Is it good?"

"Yea!" he said. "How should it not be good? So the nightin-gale calls no more from the valley-bed. But where wilt thou bear the child, for I am naked of all but life."

"We will stay here," she said.

"But the lady your mother?"

A shadow crossed her brow. She did not answer.

"What when she knows?" he said.

"She begins to know."

"And would she hurt you?"

"Ah, not me! What I have is all my own. And I shall be big with Osiris.—But thou, do thou watch her slaves."

She looked at him, and the peace of her maternity was troubled by anxiety.

"Let not your heart be troubled!" he said. "I have died the death once."

So he knew the time was come again, for him to depart. He would go alone, with his destiny. Yet not alone, for the touch would be upon him, even as he left his touch on her. And invisible suns would go with him.

Yet he must go. For here on the bay the little life of jealousy and property was resuming sway again, as the suns of passionate fecundity relaxed their sway. In the name of property, the widow and her slaves would seek to be revenged on him for the bread he had eaten, and the living touch he had established, the woman he had delighted in. But he said: Not twice! They shall not twice lay hands on me. They shall not now profane the touch in me. My wits against theirs.

So he watched. And he knew they plotted. So he moved from the little cave, and found another shelter, a tiny cove of sand by the sea, dry and secret under the rocks.

He said to the woman:

"I must go now soon. Trouble is coming to me from the slaves. But I am a man, and the world is open. But what is between us is good, and is established. Be at peace. And when the nightingale calls again from your valley-bed, I shall come again, sure as spring."

She said:

"Oh don't go! Stay with me on the half-island, and I will build a house for you and me under the pine-trees by the temple, where we can live apart."

Yet she knew that he would go. And even she wanted the coolness of her own air around her, and the release from anxiety.

"If I stay," he said, "they will betray me to the Romans and to their justice. But I will never be betrayed again. So when I am gone, live in peace with the growing child. And I shall come again; all is good between us, near or apart. The suns come back in their seasons. And I shall come again."

"Do not go yet," she said. "I have set a slave to watch at the neck of the peninsula. Do not go yet, till the harm shows."

But as he lay in his little cove, on a calm, still night, he heard the soft knock of oars, and the bump of a boat against the rock. So he crept out to listen. And he heard the Roman overseer say:

"Lead softly to the goats' den. And Lysippus shall throw the net over the malefactor while he sleeps, and we will bring him before justice, and the Lady of Isis shall know nothing of it . . . ."

The man who had died caught the whiff of flesh from the oiled and naked slaves as they crept up, then the faint perfume from the Roman. He crept nearer to the sea. The slave who sat in the boat, sat motionless, holding the oars, for the sea was quite still. And the man who had died knew him.

So out of the deep cleft of a rock he said, in a small clear voice:

"Art thou not that slave who possessed the maiden under the eyes of Isis? Art thou not the youth? Speak!"

The youth stood up in the boat in terror. His movement sent the boat bumping against the rock. The slave sprang out in wild fear, and fled up the rocks. The man who had died quickly seized the boat and stepped in, and pushed off. The oars were yet warm with the unpleasant warmth of the hands of slaves. But the man pulled slowly out, to get into the current which set down the coast, and would carry him in silence. The high coast was utterly dark against the starry night. There was no glimmer from the peninsula: the priestess came no more at night. The man who had died rowed slowly on, with the current, and laughed to himself: I have sowed the seed of my life and my resurrection, and put my touch forever upon the choice woman of this day, and I carry her perfume in my flesh like essence of roses. She is dear to me in the middle of my being. But the gold and flowing serpent is coiling up again, to sleep at the root of my tree. So let the boat carry me. Tomorrow is another day.

61

LETTERS RELATING TO
THE ESCAPED COCK

CORRESPONDENTS

THE HONORABLE DOROTHY BRETT—a painter, first met Lawrence in 1915. She is the daughter of 2nd Viscount Esher. She left England and joined the Lawrences in Taos in 1924; her last meeting with Lawrence was on Capri in 1926. She has painted several portraits of Lawrence.

MARIA CRISTINA CHAMBERS—Mrs. Chambers was born in Mexico. She was at one time an editor of the *Literary Digest*. She also attempted to help Lawrence with his American publications.

HARRY AND CARESSE CROSBY—owners and operators of The Black Sun Press, Paris, which published Lawrence's *Sun* (1928) and *The Escaped Cock* (1929). Harry Crosby was the nephew of J. P. Morgan. He committed suicide in New York in 1929. Caresse Crosby has written a vivid memoir, *The Passionate Years*. Lawrence wrote an "Introduction" for Harry Crosby's volume of poetry, *Chariot of the Sun*.

ENID HILTON—daughter of an old Eastwood friend of Lawrence's youth, William Edward Hopkin. She assisted Lawrence by typing his manuscripts and also with the then risky distribution of *Lady Chatterley's Lover* in England.

CHRISTINE HUGHES—a friend of Lawrence's from his stay in New Mexico.

WILLARD "SPUD" JOHNSON—a New Mexico friend of Lawrence's. Johnson edited the *Laughing Horse*, a lively journal which published several contributions by Lawrence. Accompanied Lawrence on one of his Mexico trips.

CHARLES LAHR—London publisher. Lawrence and Lahr once planned to edit together a satirical magazine, *The Squib*. Lahr published an edition of Lawrence's late poems, *Pansies*, and was interested in publishing *The Escaped Cock*.

HENRY GODDARD LEACH—one of the editors of *The Forum* which published Lawrence's short story "The Escaped Cock".

HARRY MARKS—New York bookseller and friend of the Crosbys. He published privately the first American edition of *The Escaped Cock*.

GIUSEPPE "PINO" ORIOLI—the Florence publisher who brought out the first edition of *Lady Chatterley's Lover*. He also published some of Lawrence's Italian translations.

EDWARD TITUS—assisted Lawrence with a number of matters toward the end of Lawrence's life. He was largely responsible for the Paris popular edition of *Lady Chatterley's Lover*.

I.

TO CHRISTINE HUGHES

Villa Mirenda
Scandicci
(Firenze)
Monday 25 April 1927

Dear Christine,

How are you by now? No news of your coming to Florence, so I expect you haven't yet let the flat. What a curse those things are.

We are going on as usual. Frieda's daughter Barbara stays until May 3rd—a week tomorrow—then goes back to London. She's supposed to paint, but hasn't done anything yet. I tell her, she's nearly as discontented and hard to please as Mary Christine, who is a tough nut in that respect. What *does* ail the young? I, who am hard boiled enough, am ten times as easy to amuse.

I've been doing a story of the Resurrection—what sort of a man "rose up", after all that other pretty little experience. Rather devastating!

The publisher is harrying me for that essay on Verga. Either a publisher is so dilatory, you think he's dead: or in such a hurry, you think he's taken salts.—I am awfully disappointed not to have heard from you, or from de Bosis or Santellana—where I can find material about Giovanni Verga—some sort of *personal* facts—and some decent *Italian* critique. I scour Florence, but Verga had better have been a Hottentot, the Italians would know more about him. I suppose I'll have to invent it out of my own head—povero me! I wish I knew someone who had *known* Verga—he only died five years ago.

Well, we are here, wherever you are. And it's nearly May!—Let me know your plans and your achievements.

Yrs., D. H. Lawrence

II.

TO HENRY GODDARD LEACH

Villa Mirenda
Scandicci
Florence Italy
22 Novem[ber] 1927

Dear Mr Leach

I'm glad you are trying *The Escaped Cock* on your public. After all, you don't cater exclusively for flappers and self-opinionated old ladies—and it *is* a good story. I do hope to goodness the Forum will manage to nucleate what is otherwise an amorphous mass of intelligent people who want a little fresh air. The mass of magazines seem to me almost asphyxiatingly stuffy—the mind simply becomes stupefied by them. I do think the Forum is trying to open a window, and if people once begin to breathe fresh air, they'll want to go on.

So here's luck—and best wishes from my wife and me—

Yours Sincerely D. H. Lawrence

III.

TO DOROTHY BRETT

[Châlet Beau Site]
Les Diablerets
[Vaud, Switzerland]
6 March 1928

Dear Brett

I am leaving here in the morning, going back to the Villa Mirenda for about six weeks. Here the snow is all going slushy—warmish spring weather, snow an anachronism. It's time to go down. The Mirenda ends finally on May 6th—so we'll be out by end of April, I expect. But I'm afraid my novel will keep me longer in Italy. At last I have the complete typescript—have posted a more-or-less expurgated script to London & to New York, each, for Secker & Knopf. Now I go to Florence with the unexpurgated. Let's hope I have luck there.—But I doubt if the thing can possibly be ready before end of May, so I'll have to stay and see it born.—It's a novel of sex: you'll probably hate it. Maria loved it: Aldous liked it, Juliette went into a white moral fury. So there you are.

Frieda says she won't come to America this summer—says my broncs aren't good enough for the long travel. But she says she *will* come early next year: and I believe the Brewsters will come too: & Aldous & Maria firmly declare they'll come with us. So that's that. It's a long time. But this seediness of mine started in Oaxaca, & has had a long course to run. I feel at last it's beginning to heal from underneath, so if it will, what do a few more months in Europe matter. At the ranch, it only healed superficially. It broke down the minute I got to New York.

You must be having a rare job with your teeth. Tell me if it really really really makes a big difference. If it does, I'll think about *three* of mine—big back ones—that might possibly be doing me harm. But I'm a bit sceptical.

Don't accumulate a lot of bills. They'll only make your life a misery. But *do tell me* if there is anything I ought to pay.

About *The Escaped Cock,* I don't really mind if Spud prints it. I had thought myself it might make a nice little private-edition thing. But I had an idea I might add on to it perhaps another 5000 words. Of course I don't know if I could. I haven't yet seen the thing in print—my copy of *The Forum* will be in Italy.—But that wouldn't prevent Spud from beginning, if he likes. Tell him to write me his idea in detail. And I suppose we'd have to tell Curtis Brown, & let him take his 10% of my share. Spud could write himself to

> Edwin G. Rich
> Curtis Brown Ltd
> 116 West 39th St. New York City

By the way, the English Curtis Brown is

> 6 Henrietta St. *Covent Garden* W.C. 2.

and not Strand.

Frieda is in Baden this last week—I alone in this little chalet, but lunch & tea with Juliette and her mother & children in the other chalet. Aldous & Maria have gone off to London. Diablerets is almost at an end. Juliette sends you many greetings.

Your paintings sound nice: hope Bobby proves a saleswoman. I wonder what I'll do with my pictures when I leave the Mirenda. And I wonder when I'll start painting again. I've gone clean off it.

Perhaps in Italy I'll start & do the rest of my Etruscan Sketches. Did you, by the way, see "Travel," with the four *Sketches of Etruscan Places* which they printed? I think it's in the Oct. Novem. Decem. & January numbers. But the illustrations were disappointing.

Remember me to Mabel & Spud and everybody. I'll write again from Italy.

D.H.L.

IV.

TO WILLARD JOHNSON

Villa Mirenda
Scandicci
(Florence)
3 June 1928

Dear Spud

Thanks for yours.—First & foremost, *don't* print *The Escaped Cock* as my agents say Crosby Gaige will put it in his privately-printed list & give me $1000. If he will, so much the better, & I can give you something else, if you like.

I shall tell Orioli to send [*MS torn*] three copies of the novel—one for you, one for Joe [   ]—remember me to him—& the other for [   ]ne's first wife. When they come, will [   ]lect the money & hand it over to [   ] pay horses feed & so on.—If only [   ]ure they'd come in, I'd send you [   ]d copies to hold.—The English have subscribed their five hundred, but the Americans not very many. I suppose they don't know.

We leave here end of this week, for French Alps or Switzerland. Write me: c/o Curtis Brown, 6 Henrietta St., W.C. 2—Glad you have a house & a press. I expect we shall turn up during the autumn, then we must do some things together.

Affectionately D. H. Lawrence

V.

TO DOROTHY BRETT

Kesselmatte
Gsteig b. Gstaad
(Bern) Switzerland
20 July 1928

Dear Brett

Here we sit in this little chalet about 4000 ft. up. It is a pleasant little place, very peaceful—and the house is very nice, so attractive inside, with the plain scrubbed wood everywhere—about 200 years old. It's a bit like the ranch—but I wish the ranch-houses were so nicely floored & walled.—You must have been doing a lot—what with your cellar and the bridge for the stream—and you seem to have a regular Pueblo of Indians up there. However do you feed them all?—especially as you say it's been so hot. But I suppose it makes it easier that you can go down to Taos for week-ends.

The Brewsters are still in the hotel in the village. They come sweating up to tea—& sometimes Earl comes & paints in the morning. I try to do just little things—small little panels—but I haven't got much art in me here. Perhaps it's just as well—as the chief thing is my health. I can't come to America, I can't really go anywhere, while my cough is as bad as it is. It's really very trying—and I can't climb hills to save my life. It all makes me feel a bit sick of things. So now I must stay here about three months and see if this won't make a real change for the better. It's really very nice & peaceful here—but of course I wouldn't have come to Swiss mountains for *choice*. They aren't my spirit's home, by any means.

I hope you have the book by now. A whole batch has been sent off to America. I hear quite a lot of people have got their copies in England—but silence about the contents, except Kot thinks it is a pity I ever published such a book. I don't think so.

My pictures have gone off to Dorothy Warren. I told you she fixed her exhibition for Oct. 4th—& the pictures were to be in New York, all of them, by Nov. 1st. I do hope that'll do. You are doing a lot of work—and lately I'm doing nothing. But I suppose there'll be enough.

I send fifty dollars for horses & taxes etc. And Spud will give you another thirty when he gets the three copies of Lady C.—I haven't raked in much yet—most people haven't paid for the copies they've ordered, & they won't, till they get them.—And I haven't given Crosby Gaige the second half of *Escaped Cock,* though I've written it, & I think it's lovely. But somehow I don't want to let it go out of my hands. It lies here in MS.—not typed yet.—I've done a few newspaper articles to keep the pot boiling.—A man wrote from Taos wanting to buy the ranch for $2000—but I said we weren't selling just now. I must anyhow see it again. Hope you're having a good summer.

D.H.L.

VI.

TO ENID HILTON

Kesselmatte
Gsteig b. Gstaad
(Bern)
Tuesday [?28 August 1928]

Dear Enid

The Aldingtons are going off to Italy for the winter on Friday. I asked them, if they have any Lady Cs left, to send them to you. They may have about five copies.

Can you type—& have you got a typewriter? If so, would you do me a story—about 10,000 words—which I don't quite care to send to the professional typist? I'll pay the proper rates, of course.

Emily & her daughter are here—and today it's pouring rain. They stay till Friday week. I expect we shall leave on Sept. 15th—or thereabouts.

I had your last letter & list of all you sent. I do wish we'd never sent any to R.A. Kot is such a fusser. Hope all goes peacefully.

tante cose! D. H. L.

VII.
TO MARIA CRISTINA CHAMBERS

[Hotel Löwen
Lichtenthal b.]
Baden-Baden
26 Sept[ember] 1928

Dear Mrs Chambers

Your letter came on this morning from Florence. Orioli says he received it with the seals broken, and opened. So who is reading your mail?

I must say the American attitude to Lady C. is rather disgusting. The English are bad enough, but still there's quite a lot of intelligent appreciation there—even enthusiastic. Whereas all the Americans either squirm & look sickly, or become sordidly indignant. Anyhow I'm glad you put in a blow or two for the Lady.—You got your two cheques back safely, I presume. Orioli isn't sending any copies to U.S.A.—but there is talk that a man in New York will print 1000 copies for private subscription. I don't know if it will come off—and don't care either. If you happen to go into the Skylark Bookshop in New York, find out if they had their three copies sent them—but don't put yourself to any trouble, and *don't* run athwart the precious authorities.

I told you we shan't come to America this year—and I shan't send my pictures. So the show in London will be a little later—I suppose November—and I shan't go there either. I am leaving here next week for the south of France, to join some friends there. Germany doesn't make me feel happy this time—though it seems very prosperous. But it chills something in one's marrow—or one's soul.

I finished *The Escaped Cock*—with a second half in which there is the real resurrection of the flesh. An American said he wanted to do a limited edition of it. I don't suppose he will. But I don't care at all—I can do it myself.

At present I feel a bit of special disgust with the civilised human species—especially the Transatlantic section of it. *So* unclean and ignominious. So absolutely unbrave.

But patience! patience!

D. H. Lawrence

VIII.

Hotel Beau Rivage
Bandol
Var [France]
Sat. 2 March 1929

Dear Pino,

We are staying here a day or two longer—no use hurrying away from this warm hotel, while the cold weather lasts—it has come back a bit, but not so bad. But I think we shall go on Wednesday to Marseilles, and then to Spain. I think Spain would be more fun than Corsica, at least for a while—and it's really not far from here.

I'm glad those two copies to Conway of Mexico City were not lost. The Mexican mail should be quite safe—has nothing to do with U.S.A. Have you sent them off now?—and the one to the man in Germany? I hear Lahr has sold one or two copies—five or six, really—of the first edition, but he's not paid in the money yet. What a pity he hasn't got more! I wish Brentanos would pay for those ten, then the second edit. is all paid, and I could send you your share.

I suppose you have heard of all the fuss with Jix. I don't know if there is any result yet. Did you see this cartoon from the Evening Standard? I'm getting very bored with the whole silly show.

The Crosby Gaige man drew up a contract for the first half of *Escaped Cock*—in which I promise not to issue the second half till 1930. But I wrote back saying he must put in a clause: that the title must be *The Escaped Cock. Part One*—and that at the end he must put: *Here ends the First Part of the Escaped Cock.*—That puts salt on *his* tail. He's hanging fire—not answered yet. If he backs out, I don't care—then we'll do the whole thing for Easter 1930—it would just make a nice book for you to do, about sixty pages. And next year let us hope we can post again to England pretty freely.—The Pegasus Press turned down the *Lady C.* proposition: now I have written to Mr. Moulder of Galignani. I hear the pirated edit. is on sale in Nice at 400 frs! Shame that no one would tackle a Paris edit.—I got the blue coat from Maria—it's the very same I tried on last year in the shop, a bit *small*, with the golden buttons—but it will do.—I wonder where we shall ultimately settle! At the moment I feel very undecided about everything. I shall send an address as soon as I have one—then write me. Love from us both.

D.H.L.

IX.

TO HARRY AND CARESSE CROSBY

[Hotel de Versailles]
60 Bvd. Montparnasse
Paris
4 April 1929

Dear Harry & Caresse

I was sorry I couldn't come in yesterday—a set of complications—
but I know, Caresse, you were so busy anyhow, you'd be glad to escape
me.

I got the enclosed leaflet from Philadelphia. These people must be
pirating *your* edition of *Sun*. But since the story is copyright in my vol.
of short stories *The Woman Who Rode Away* (Alfred Knopf 1928) we
can prosecute them & get them into prison. I must do this, or they'll
pirate my very beard. Only I'm wondering how best to set about it.

We must make very sure of the copyright of *The Escaped Cock*. The
first part of the story was printed in the *Forum,* New York, in the
spring of 1928. Does that secure permanent copyright? We must find
out. If not we must have a small edition of the first part printed in New
York—say about 50 copies at 2 dollars each & get the copyright on
that. If you have read the story, & like it, & still want to print it, you
might think about this, & perhaps speak of it to your man Marks (your
New York bookseller). For the whole story, I think, if you copyright it
in France, under the Berne Convention, it holds good for England. We
will make sure. I *must* protect myself from pirates. You see another 1500
edit. of Lady C. at 15 dollars—over $20,000 for a new lot of rogues.
I am sick of it.

Please don't lose that little leaflet. We must trace that pirate.

My grippe came back on me a bit—but I am getting tickets to leave
for Spain on Sunday morning. Hope you are not inundated by family
feeling.

All good luck.

Affectionately D. H. Lawrence

X.

TO HARRY AND CARESSE CROSBY

Hotel Royal
Palma de Mallorca
Baleares, España
18 April 1929

Dear Harry & Caresse

Well here we are on Majorca—& those brilliant incandescent blue mornings of the Southern Mediterranean that I know so well from Sicily —something eternally new & dawn-like. But this island, at least here, doesn't seem *beautiful* like Sicily—It has a certain forever asleepness which is also utterly dull, but which has too the charm of the sleep trance. I think we shall stay a while, & I think it will do me good, body & soul—sleep, the sweet sleep!—and the trance of islands that lie in the sun, and cannot be ravished out of the sun.

I wonder how you got along with your father, and how Berlin affected you. I should think it was nervous excitation & exasperation all the while—the reverse of here, where the people still haven't reached the stage of having nerves, & where, at first, one is exasperated by the sheer absence of nervous tension. It is almost like falling down a clear, calm hole: & landing on sheer dulness. But not really dull, as the little boats go out past the mole, so white in the asleep afternoon: & somehow up-lifted.

Curtis Brown's said they were sending you the other copy of *Escaped Cock*: so you will keep it safe for me. I discovered the MS. of the first part in my bag—& I know where the MS. of the second part is, in London. If you are the first to print the thing, then you must have the MSS. too. But I won't send them now to Florence to be bound—safer not risk too much postage.

I do hope you are feeling easy & not all upset. Many greetings from us both.

D.H.L.

XI.

TO CARESSE CROSBY

Hotel Principe Alfonso
Palma de Mallorca
Spain
17 May 1929

Dear Caresse Crosby

Too bad that it's still chilly at the Mill—I like to think of the court-yard flooded with sunshine, & a few bright daffodils sparkling. Here it goes on being sunny, but sometimes the wind is cool almost to chill. It hasn't rained for months.

It's rather nice—but I don't think I want to live here. There's a certain deadness. I think in about a fortnight we'll take the boat to Marseilles, & go to Italy. Frieda is still lamenting for a house, so I suppose we'd better go and look for one. So we shan't be here in July to receive you & your party on a yacht—staggering thought—though perhaps we may see you somewhere else, for I don't expect we shall go very far away. The yacht sounds thrilling—whose is it?

And how did your race-party go off?—and did you ride the She-ass of the first order?—I hope you've got her. I expect you'll end by having a strange & wonderful collection of asses, striped ones & plain, pale & dark, in the effort to come at the right article: & they'll get uppish, & rove around like lions.

I think the *Escaped Cock* MS. is all right. Curtis Brown now has it in his safe in London, & says every post he is sending it to you, but hangs on to it in order to prevent my publishing it. He doesn't know I've got a duplicate. In my next I'll tell him to send it *at once*: though I don't divulge any plans. They were at me again to let the Fountain Press, or whatever it is, publish Part I. separately, and I again said no! Persistent as the devil they are, to try to prevent one having anything done apart from *them*.

I have had proofs of twenty or so of my pictures—reproductions—some not bad, some to weep over. They talk of getting that book out by the end of the month.

Hope you are both cheerful & calm. Keep us posted as to your plans.

belle cose! D.H.L.

XII.

TO HARRY CROSBY

Hotel Principe Alfonso
Palma de Mallorca
Spain
20 May 1929

Dear Harry

Yours today—and didn't I give you the *complete* MS. of *Escaped Cock?*—was it only the second half? Curtis Brown, the old devil doesn't forward the full typescript—ask Caresse would she mind writing him as follows—"Mr Lawrence asked me to take charge of the complete MS. of Escaped Cock, and I am a little anxious that it does not turn up. Will you please tell me if you have sent it already, or if you are sending it." That'll get it out of him. Meanwhile I send you my handwritten MS. of the first part, which I found in my bag, & which I want you to accept from me as a small gift.—Then further I shall have sent to you the written MS. of the second part, which also please accept from me, together with *corrected typescript* of first part. These are in the hands of a reliable friend in London, but she is in S. of France for another week, I believe—then going back. It would be well to print from this corrected typescript—but you can begin from my handwritten script, because only the end is changed just a trifle. That is, if you want. (When I look at the MS. I find it is rather mixed—I can't remember exactly what I did with it. Of course one could easily get a copy of *The Forum,* containing the story: spring 1928. But the MS will come from London.)

I wrote Caresse & hope she had it. I think we shall try & make a little tour in Spain, if my health holds up—it's pretty good here—and then sail Barcelona to Genoa—Frieda does want a house—& in Italy— so we'd better go & find one. But we shan't go far from the sea, so do sail & see us—fun!

Good that Constance—la Comtesse—has her divorce—but tell her to spend a year in contemplation before she starts marrying again. Marriage is a treacherous stimulant.

It's all summer here, so the restlessness of spring has gone by. I find I can be very successfully lazy—in fact I don't do a thing but eat and sleep and chatter.—Allanah Harper sounded—in letters—so brisk, that I'm surprised she has faded out. As for the four seas, that's too many— get your MS. back & do it *Narcisse.* I hate *all* publishers—& agents.

Hope you are serene—with all the asses & lasses, Narcisse & Caresses

D.H.L.

75

Frieda would love a little gramophone but *no* Joyce,—and please, not till we get a house—don't give us a single thing, not even a book, not a post-card, while we are still living in & out of bags.

D.H.L.

XIII.

ENID HILTON TO CARESSE CROSBY

44 Mecklenburgh Square
London W.C. 1
7.6.29

Dear Madame.

As instructed by Mr. D. H. Lawrence, I have today sent by registered letter post, the manuscript of his story "The Escaped Cock". This is in two parts, the first part being in type and the second in manuscript.

If, after a reasonable period, this has not reached you, will you kindly let me know?

Yours faithfully, Enid Hilton

XIV.

TO HARRY AND CARESSE CROSBY

Hotel Principe Alfonso
Palma de Mallorca
Spain
7 June 1929

Dear Harry & Caresse

You see we are still here—keep putting off leaving—now we say we'll catch the boat on the 18th.

I hear you have got the complete MS of *Escaped Cock* from Curtis Brown: and probably by now the original MS. of the second part, from Mrs Hilton. With the latter must be my typescript of the first part, which I did myself, with alterations & additions, from the handwritten MS. of the first part which I sent you. So now you will have all the original MSS. of *Escaped Cock* & I want you to keep them in memory of the Black Sun Press edition.—Curtis Brown wants me to publish a book of short stories in September, and to include in it the first part of *Escaped Cock*. I am inclined to do it, as it secures copyright of at least so much. And a public edition will not hurt our edition: & you might possibly get yours out first. What do you think? If you copyright the whole thing in Paris, under the Berne Convention law, that covers England, but not U.S.A. Tell me how many copies you think of printing—I suppose five hundred. I have a bookseller in London who no doubt would take 150 or 250, if we could get them over to him. He is very reliable. And if Marks takes the others for U.S.A., then there is no advertising or canvassing to be done.—I suppose the price will be ten dollars or two guineas.

So much for business. My book of pictures is just about ready—and will go all right if the police don't start interfering again. I would send you a copy, but I feel perhaps you don't want it. I believe you won't like my pictures. Too concrete, too physical. But I like them. Then the poems *Pansies* are coming out this month, but I shan't send you a copy of the public edition, as a little later I am bringing out a private limited edition (secret) and I shall give you a copy of that, because it is unexpurgated & complete and I believe you'll like some of the poems. The public edition is expurgated.

How long are you staying now in Paris? Let me know.

I knew that big horse of yours wouldn't run—his flanks are the wrong shape. He's no go. The little one will be better, if you enter him right. Those stable people of course will always tell you lies—a stranger might get a hint of their real opinion from them.

The Moulin must be a god-send now the hot weather is come—the forest so near—and real good donkeys to drive out with, or to ride. That must be fun. And *where* is the swimming pool?—When a man has nothing to do, how hard it is for him to do nothing! You ought, you know, to be a fighter. There's such a lot of things you could go for, tooth and nail, if you would. With life as it is today, the battle is everything. But of course if you don't really believe in anything, there's nothing to fight for. Anyhow Heliogabalus is all bunk—he was so bored he went cracked, out of boredom.

Lovely weather here—& such hot sun—but the air is cool. You'd be cooked as brown as a brioche, on this little beach.

Caresse, write us a line & tell us *your* side of the news. You are dead silent lately. I hope you haven't lost your heart entirely to the Comte—or is it Vicomte?—at the Mill. You'd never be able to pay his bills. And is he still handsome? (absolutely red-faced and stupid) and virile (fat, and *quite* a lump) and does he respond to Harry's challenging cannon-shot with wild caterwaulings from the Château? If not, he ought.

Au revoir, mes chers, soyez deux petits anges.

D.H.L.

XV.

TO CHARLES LAHR

Hotel Löwen
Lichtenthal
Baden-Baden
8 August 1929

Dear Lahr

The poems in the case came today—but how did you send them, because my wife had to go to the Zollamt for them, and they asked if it was anything political. Asses! I like the case all right—and I'm glad you can insert that page, it makes the copy that came today much better. But the crowding of the pages is still rather a grief to me—though I don't want to seem ungrateful, you've been awfully good doing all the work, and I'm glad to see the book in existence. Will you mark the other non-Secker poems?

About the green vellum—if I choose a green it will [be] sure to be one that doesn't exist in vellum. Could you perhaps send me one or two patterns?—I can send them all back if necessary.

Pouring with rain—and Thursday evening, the fate of the pictures should be decided by now. A sad sort of evening. I don't feel very happy in Germany.

Don't send me any more copies of the poems—you've sent me No. 13 & No. 15. Perhaps you can send the other gift copies "out of series" & unnumbered. You could write inside: Out of series—for Max Mohr—& so on: Out of Series: for Enid Hilton. Then you would have all the numbered copies for sale.

I do hope there'll be no fuss.—I am so tired of the nonsense.

The Black Sun Press in Paris—you had one of their books—is doing a story of mine for the autumn—The Escaped Cock—an important story. They are doing 450 copies & 50 on vellum, and are sending them all to New York: none to England. I shall send you a set of proofs. Perhaps we might do that next, for England. It is a longish story: I care a good deal about it: about 100 pp. I am doing water-colour decorations for this Paris edition. What do you think of it? It is no use for public editions—but nothing terrible.

Well now we must wait & see if all goes well with the hearts-ease. Next year my nettles.

I shall ask Secker to send review copies to the Sunday Worker—little snob. But you'll see, the socialists will hate me most of all. I should like to see real Labour or Socialist or red reviews of Pansies: of which, by the way, I am asking Secker to bring out a cheap edition—but it depends also on that damned slow Knopf. He won't want to be undersold. Secker wants to do a 7/6 Collected Poems, but Cape is still selling at 5 dollars—so impossible yet.

Well you know I'm really grateful to you for doing the book for me.

D.H.L.

XVI.

TO CARESSE CROSBY

Hotel Löwen
Lichtenthal
Baden-Baden
12 Aug[ust] 1929

Dear Caresse

I have done the four small bits of decoration for the Cock, & have nearly finished the frontispiece—shall send them along soon. But I was wondering about your edition. Why don't you print 750?—and let Marks have 500, and keep 250 to dispose of this side? I don't see why Marks should have the monopoly. And do please tell me what price he is going to charge—it should be at least $10—and what terms does he make with you? He ought, of course, to pay you $6.65 for each $10.- copy—and no bookseller would take more than 40%—which means he would give you $6 on a $10 copy. What are his terms? Have you already fixed them? This is a book that will soon be snapped up—why give it away to Harry Marks? Then I suppose you halve profits with me— was that your intention? Write me a business letter with all details, we may as well have it all square. What I don't see, is why all copies should go to New York. Why should not some be sold in Europe?

Anyhow let me know, and I will send some proofs & decorations. We shall be here some time still.

I heard from Forte from Maria Huxley—no sign so far of any gramophone.

How is Harry?

D.H.L.

XVII.

TO CARESSE CROSBY

Hotel Löwen
Lichtenthal
Baden-Baden
15 Aug[ust] 1929

Dear Caresse

Here are the décors for the Cock, & the corrected proofs go off by the same mail, but as imprimés. I hope you'll like the decorations—I almost wish I had done the frontispiece in two colours only, it will be so tiresome to reproduce. You might ask the colour-printers how it would come out in the same green & red as the other things. For the little tail-pieces, choose whatever you like & the things will reduce to proportion. The little round head-pieces will need to be reduced to about the size of the ring I drew at the head of Part I.

What about the copyright? It is really important to secure it, or this story will be at once pirated, in U.S.A. anyhow. Do you think it would be any good to print on [it *deleted*] Part I: This story has appeared in the American *Forum?*

For getting the thing into America, that also might help.—Or you might try sending in sheets—& if they go through, then the bindings and the frontispiece, & let the book be bound up in N. York. Are you going to have those cases again? They don't seem very necessary to me.

And don't let Marks sell to the public under $10 a copy, really. You see the other things I bring out privately are that price.—And don't let him rook you. I am so used to being rooked by booksellers et al., that I'm sick of it, and on the defensive.

Well anyhow I hope you'll like the decorations. Let me know. And I hope things are going smoothly.

No sound of gramophone, or anything for Italy. Pazienza!

I like the look of the book very much—think you've made a nice thing of it.

Love from both to both

D.H.L.

It is Marias Himmelfahrt—Maria's Ascension to heaven—today: the bells are ringing for her departure. I say *bon voyage*—but not *au revoir*. Goodbye dear, but don't come back!

XVIII.

TO EDWARD TITUS

Hotel Löwen
Lichtenthal
Baden-Baden
16 Aug[ust] 1929

Dear Titus

Your letter this morning, and the cheque for francs 3810—which as you say, is not so bad. Who was it, by the way, let you down in the first place? I like to know who is reliable & who isn't. The Gotham Book Mart, by the way, tried hard to let me down over Lady C.—I hope Random House or somebody will send me a copy of the Skirmish— surely I am due to have a copy. It seems to me they figure very low when they expect their profits to be only $200 or $300, selling out the whole 600 copies. If it is so, they've chucked money away rarely on production.

There is no Paris *Pansies* as far as I know. You are aware, of course, that Secker's public edition has been out in London a month—and sold about 3000 copies at 10/6, last time I heard—so the pirates would hardly tackle that. But what there is—and I wanted it kept secret —is a little edition of 500, printed & produced in London—coming out in London just now. It is printed unexpurgated & complete from the original confiscated MS.—& is to sell at £2. I believe it is all ordered. But I shall try to send you a copy. I have to keep quiet about it as the police are getting fierce because I defy them.—Another thing that is coming in Paris is a long short story—about 100 pp.—which the Crosbys are doing on their Black Sun Press—500 copies. But I believe they are shipping the whole 500 *en bloc* to New York, which seems a pity. Why not have some to sell in Europe!—I arranged this with them before I knew you, so it can't be a *casus belli*.

I haven't a word from Curtis Brown's office lately, most of them are away holidaying. But I will write & ask about the Gallimard contract, and let you know.

I haven't thanked you for the copy of *Lady C.* and *This Quarter,* safely received.

We are staying on here, as it is very pleasant. Hope you'll have a [pleasant *deleted*] nice change (can't write, people talking to me all the time).

Sincerely   D. H. Lawrence

XIX.

CARESSE CROSBY TO D.H.L.

[19 rue de Lille]
Paris
August 27th, 1929

Dear Lorenzo,

The proofs and watercolors came, the book will be marvellous! Thank
you so much. Only we will probably have to send the frontispiece over
separately to be put in there. Mr. Marks says they are getting stricter
and stricter and more and more troublesome at the Douane. Since I had
your letter I wrote him to ask him about prices for he had just sailed. I
am sure I can sell to him high enough so that we will clear considerably
more than I told you in my last letter—of course it will sell wonder-
fully, only he does have to give ⅓ off to the bookshops and pay 25%
duties and tax de luxe as well, so that the book must retail for *over* twice
as much as I sell to him for and I have to consider that in making my
prices—at any rate it will be $10 retail at least for the regular copies.

I will be able to send you an advance copy about the middle of
September.

When are you coming back to the Mill?

Love from Caresse

P.S. As soon as I have definite figures as to cost of publication and
sales price I will let you know exactly what the book will net you.
Love to Frieda.   C.

XX.

TO CARESSE CROSBY

Kaffee Angermaier
Rottach-am-Tegernsee
Oberbayern [Bavaria]
9 Sept[ember] 1929

Dear Caresse

Your letter came on in time, & I had your telegram. Glad you liked
the pictures, but I still wish I had done a sort of plain one for the front.

I want you particularly to tell me what you are doing about copyright.
It is very important to secure it, at least for the continent of Europe, &

if possible, provisionally for America. Please don't overlook it.

Will you print me half a dozen out of series copies, to give away to friends?

And what about the sheets to sign?

We want to leave here in about another week or so, & go south to Italy, perhaps a short while to Venice, then to Florence. Shall let you know exactly. But if you have sheets you want me to sign, can't you get them to me here?

How are you both? and how are Harry's loves? One can only speak of them, like his drinks, in the plural. And how is Narcisse? and the ânes sang-pur? It must be lovely at the Mill now. Lovely here, but of course I've been in bed with a chest. I don't really like mountains, so I think they don't like me.

belle cose!   D. H. Lawrence

XXI.

TO CARESSE CROSBY

[Kaffee Angermaier]
Rottach-Egern
[Oberbayern, Bavaria]
16 Sept[ember] 1929

Dear Caresse

I have signed & numbered 50 vellum sheets, & signed six extra in case of accident—packed them up as they came—and now I hope they will reach you safely and without damage. I shall have them sent off to-morrow.

I am very anxious to see the book, & so is Frieda. I wish you had sent me proofs of the colour reproductions—I expect you have them by now.

I am thinking, perhaps when Marks has sold this edition—which ought to take only a very short time—he might make another, cheaper edition, without pictures, and copyright in the ordinary way. He could hold this cheaper edition back a few months, if he liked, the copyright secured. And he could make an agreement direct with me. This would save us from pirates, and would be to his interest.—Otherwise I might get another publisher in America to take it up. Have you any objection to a cheaper American edition appearing, say, in November? Don't forget to let me know about this.

If the printers spoil too many copies in press—or colour-process—then save me some of the imperfect copies, they will do at a pinch to give away.

And I think I shall have to arrange for an English edition immediately yours is gone—have you any objection?

We are leaving here on Wednesday—day after tomorrow—for South of France. I shall write immediately I have an address. But if you need to get me quickly, write c/o Thomas Cook, La Canebière, Marseille.

If it weren't such a long way up to Paris, I'd love a few sunny autumn days at the Mill. What about Madame de Jumiac, by the way?—and the red-haired man from Cannes? Did they affect a—I mean *effect*—a marriage? And how is Harry's erotic temperature?

You know, by the way, Marks can secure a temporary U.S.A. copyright (for 3 months) by sending a copy of the French edition to Washington.

Yes I should like to read the story of your eight weeks—what a mercy it's not six! I expect my hair will curl, but even if it does itself up into knots I shall stand by you. Or is it only Harry's "advice to his wife"—I hope that makes part of the eight weeks' record—which will make hair-curlers in the book (I hope it's a long book)?

Love from Frieda & from Lorenzo

D.H.L.

XXII.

CARESSE CROSBY TO D.H.L.

[19 rue de Lille
Paris]
September 23, 1929

Dear Lorenzo,

I have received the Japan sheets back again—Thank you very much for the many signatures.

I couldn't send you examples of the color because they are only now (after the printing of the text) being done and you will so soon have the completed book—I had the frontispiece interpreted in fewer colors (as you said I might) and also reduced in size so as not to overbalance the type—it will look very well and not being quite so flaming it should not offend the civil authorities!

I will write Mr. Marks your suggestion about a cheaper edition later on, but I must ask you not to have the English or the U.S. edition done until *six months* after our publication—as this has always been our agreement with Mr. Marks, and has been the case with all our other first editions (Joyce, Kay Boyle, Hart Crane) he will not have the book on sale before November, as it takes several weeks for shipment and it will be another week at least before it is ready to send.

The Gramophone is on its return trip to Paris, when can Frieda meet with it?

Harry has just shot a pheasant cock in the garden—first game of the season—with a beautiful flaming tail. They came over the fence to eat our "corn on the cob".

Best love to you both. I hope this oppression cast by the Mountains has lifted and that all is well with you.

Love from Caresse

XXIII.

TO CHARLES LAHR

Villa Beau Soleil
Bandol
Var [France]
28 Sept[ember] 1929

Dear L.

Had yours last night. All right, we'll let the poems lie.—Orioli & Douglas are moaning that they haven't received their copies. Douglas is c/o Thomas Cook, Via Tornabuoni, Florence.

Do send them if you can.—Aldous Huxley is in London for a few days—catch him if you can via Jack Hutchinson, 3 Albert Road, Regents Park and give him his *Pansies*. And ask him about the Squib.— Kot can telephone Hutchinson if you don't want to.—I know Aldington very well but don't want to write him. If the Squib *begins,* then you write and ask him for some venomous trifle, and tell him I said I wanted him to come in.—Tell Aldous the same. And I'll write him.—

I think the Squib is fun: but *no names*: all *noms de guerre* & advertise it: The most famous among the young authors, writing under *noms de plume*. A good fetch.

Do give Davies the £10.- I've got things for the Squib whenever it will be ready. Aldous is 3 rue du Bac, Suresnes, Seine. Fredk. Carter might do something.

The *Black Sun Press* edn. of *Escaped Cock* is nearly ready. They are shipping all to U.S.A.—500 copies—& expect to sell it in November— Harry B. Marks, the bookseller. But don't talk about it—the quieter the better.—They stipulate a six months interval after the first edn. But I say, if there is a threat of pirates, we must forestall them, six months or no six months. So I shall send you a set of proofs.

But I should like to wind up completely with the poems before doing another book. Do you think Stephensen has sold all those copies? And can you get him to pay, & then you send me the accounts, all settled up and finished?—All, that is, apart from these new red ones. And these we will pay for from Mandrake payments—so really all will be settled. But I shall give you 10/- on the red ones, if you think it is enough.

If the Squib starts give Davies his £10.- and another £10.- in a month's time, and if the Squib fizzles out, it's my loss. I don't want any re-payment.

I wish you would keep for me a copy of my articles & stories—news-paper stuff & magazine stuff—a copy of each thing as it appears—and charge me a bill—but keep me the things together on a shelf. Would it bore you? Or any really interesting criticisms too.

Start the Squib if you're going to—& tell me & I'll write a little edi-torial.

D.H.L.

XXIV.

TO CARESSE CROSBY

Villa Beau Soleil
Bandol
Var [France]
28 Sept[ember] 1929

Dear Caresse

Glad to hear from you, & looking forward to the book. We've taken this little house on the sea for the winter, bang in the sun. I find strong sunlight has a soothing & forgetful effect on one.

When you send the books to Marks, will you include in the shipment a gift copy from me to Mrs. Maria Cristina Chambers, & ask him to hand it over to her. Can't trust the post—so she will call on Marks with a note from me, & he can give her the book.

And will you send me his address. I must write to him about that copyright business. In six months Lady Chatterley had been pirated at least four times in U.S.A. & I lost at least $15,000. It is ridiculous for me to abstain from publishing, if the pirates are going to rush in—& rush in they will, with this story. Marks must meet the situation or leave me to handle it. Anyhow please send me his address.

And send me that lurid frontispiece to the *Cock* when the printer has done with it. I suppose you don't want to keep it?—I hope they kept the man red enough, or it loses its point.

ever D. H. Lawrence

XXV.

TO HARRY MARKS

Villa Beau Soleil
Bandol
Var [France]
28 Sept[ember] 1929

Dear Mr Marks

I asked Mrs Crosby please to include a gift copy of *The Escaped Cock* in her shipment to you. I hope the thing comes safely in—and if it does, will you please give the said gift copy to Mrs Maria Cristina Chambers, who will bring you this note.

I am anxious about the copyright of the *Cock*. I don't want the whole thing pirated from me, as *Lady Chatterley* was. The best thing would be to have a cheap edition ready to forestall the pirates—and I must do [the same *deleted*] that in England. Will you assure me that you will protect me in the United States?

Yours Sincerely   D. H. Lawrence

XXVI.

TO MARIA CRISTINA CHAMBERS

Villa Beau Soleil
Bandol
Var France
11 Oct[ober] 1929

Dear Maria Cristina

Your letters to us both today, also cheque for $100. The cheque I have torn up, as I intended you to keep those hundred dollars for your running about expenses.

So sorry about the scratched leg, & I do hope it will heal soon. Now you want your stone back. Shall I send it?

I enclose two photographs—You can get them reproduced quite cheaply at any photographers—many as you like.

Yes, your man could have any number of the Paris *Lady C* if he could get them in—there's the rub.

Yes, I had my money all right for the *Skirmish*—quite apart from Rich. And Curtis Browns in London want to handle it on this side!— But I think Mencken is right, & a magazine won't publish it now that it has appeared in an edition of 500.—I told CB.'s also about the *Vanity Fair* reproductions, & that it was my affair.—I don't think Crowninshields would mind your offering the other pictures to other people *after* his four have appeared.—He wants, through Curtis Brown, to make a contract with me to give him an essay a month—I couldn't trust myself to write one every month, I'm afraid.

I saw the review of Lady C. in New Republic—Brett sent it.—There will be a review of the book in Jan. in *Pagany* (Boston). By the way, I offered the editor "The Risen Lord" article which appeared in *Everyman,* a copy of which you will receive—& I asked him to let you know if he accepted it. (Richard Johns, 94 Revere St., Boston).

I am waiting still for a copy of *The Escaped Cock* from Paris—& for an answer to my letter. They are very high-handed, these precious little people.—Don't give my letter to Harry Marks just yet—unless you've done so—spy out his hand a bit first.

We have got this little house on the sea for six months, so the address is good. It is a rocky sea, very blue, with little islands way out, & mountains behind Toulon—still a touch of Homer, in the dawn—we like it—& it is good for my health. The Moros are setting off today for Spain in the Morrrras' [Mohrs'] car. They want to come & take a house here also in Dec!!

I do hope all goes well.

D.H.L.

XXVII.

TO CARESSE CROSBY

Villa Beau Soleil
Bandol
Var [France]
15 Oct[ober] 1929

Dear Caresse

Yes, I like it very much indeed. The picture came out very well, considering—which is luck. I do hope it goes through all right. Let me know if you hear from Marks that it is arriving safely.

I want to know how many copies you have kept for me. And surely you will give me one of the vellum copies, for myself. But I *must* have some of the others, out of series, to give away. Let me know how many I can have. Perhaps you would post me one or two from Paris? I mean, to my sisters & friends, if I sent you the address.

You didn't give me Marks' address, but I wrote him all the same. And are you enclosing that copy for Mrs Chambers, as I asked you, & telling

Marks to give it her? Please do!

I am having the book set up in London—no decorations—just an ordinary unlimited edition at, perhaps, 7/6. But I shan't release it till March or April, unless there is a pirate appearance.

The gramophone is in Florence, and will probably be sent on here—but it's quite safe.

We've got this little house till end of March, & are installed, with a decent cook. But alas, my health is so bad, it went all to pieces in Germany, and I am in bed again here, feeling pretty rotten. I expect I shall have to go into a sanatorium for a time, unless I pick up very soon. No use dying just yet. Do you know a good sanatorium on this coast?—or near Cannes or Nice? Am thoroughly miserable. Should have loved a marvellous party of celebration. But it will have to wait a bit. Anyhow we'd have to wait till we knew it was all safely landed in New York. Perhaps I'll pick up again.

Lovely weather, still sea, soft sun—I lie & look out. But I am miserable about my health.

How is Harry? how are you? Frieda is pretty well, but a wee bit lame still from a sprained foot—done in Mallorca.

D. H. Lawrence

XXVIII.

TO CHARLES LAHR

[Villa] Beau Soleil
[Bandol
Var France]
Saturday [? 9 November 1929]

Dear L.

Thanks for letter & enclosure. That's bad news of Stephensen. He wrote me that he was having to leave London to be in the country for three months, and the Mandrake would be at a standstill but he hoped it would put forth new shoots in the spring. Meanwhile he sent me a copy of Rozanov—& three more of the 3/6 series. He is afraid *Rozanov* won't sell. I wrote an article on it and sent it to Curtis Brown, but don't know if anyone will print it. I didn't think the 3/6 is very good—a W. J. Turner, & an Edgell Rickword, & a *Smiling Faces*. But I can't believe people break their necks to buy such little stuff. If *only* Stephensen weren't in such a hurry!—Tell me, do you think Goldston has *actually* sold all the painting books, & all the *Pansies?*—It is rough on Davies if the Mandrake dies, but then we'd have to publish his novels ourselves, and he'd have to sell them. He wrote to Frieda from Wales, chewing the cud of misery and rather liking the taste of it. I believe success would make him feel quite ill.— You don't tell me if you think it would be safe for me to send you the Hahn* through the post. It is quite a lovely little book—in get-up. I am still waiting to hear if it has passed through into U.S.A.—Look out for my *Obscenity & Pornography* pamphlet in Faber & Faber's series—should be out soon.—I am not in any hurry over the Goldston money & the Jackson, except that it would be nice to get the thing all finished up & done with. But please deduct your proper share, & all the costs of sending me books—like the Bible etc.—very useful. And if you can see a good translation of *Hesiod:* Homeric Hymns, Works & Days, Fragments—then please send it me. I don't know if the Loeb is the best. And if you come across a second-hand Plutarch—I think in Bohn's library—send me that. But be sure & take the money for them all from my payments.

We must discuss a plan for publishing Davies' novels, if you & he think it wise. But he would have to look after it properly.

And the Hahn we will discuss when I know it is in New York all right.—Shall I mail you a copy, reg. letter post or how?

Tell Davies to spend that £10.-, or I shall throw it in the sea.

ever D.H.L.

Have you got the *Story of Doctor Manente* from Orioli? I think it ought to sell—& absolutely "safe".

---

*Hahn: *German,* cock

XXIX.

TO CHARLES LAHR

[Villa] Beau Soleil
Bandol
Var [France]
24 Jan[uary] 1930

Dear L

I haven't written—been so seedy—now the doctor says I must lie quite still, do no work at all, see nobody, & try to get better—not even think of work. So I am obeying.

I have no further news of the Hahn: shall let you know. What was your idea about it? To do a public edition, with another title? Tell me.

Tell Davies thanks for his letter, & he must stop off here & see me—
I'm not allowed now to read an MS.—but perhaps later. Now I do
nothing but lie in bed, kaput!

D.H.L.

XXX.

TO CHARLES LAHR

Ad Astra
Vence
A.M. [France]
9 Feb[ruar]y [19]30

Dear Lahr

I have never mentioned *Escaped Cock* to Goldston—never written
him in my life—I'm afraid this is another piracy trick of his—but the
book is sheltered under the Berne convention copyright. I don't want
him to do it anyhow—after that *Pansies* affair.—I have written to Pollinger of Curtis Brown to see if he'd look after it for me—then if we can
fix up, you'd better print quickly, as I mistrust Goldston & Co. I am not
bound to those six months—we can come out in March if we like.

I like the poems by the Powys boy.

But don't do like Stephensen, too many little things one after the
other.

If I am well I think I shall come to England this summer.

D.H.L.

XXXI.

TO CHARLES LAHR

Ad Astra
Vence
A.M. [France]
20 Feb[ruary 19]30

Dear Lahr

Heard from Pollinger—he talks of making a regular contract for
Man Who had Died. (You must put *Escaped Cock* as a sub-title)—
But I don't want you to pay any money in advance—I don't want it. Pay
at the end of the first month, on all copies sold.

Titus said you could send along the 200 *Pansies,* and he would arrange selling them. But he's very indefinite.

If you do publish *Man Who Had Died,* get it out as soon as possible, will you.

I'm rather worse in this beastly place—

ever **D.H.L.**

XXXII.
FRIEDA LAWRENCE TO CARESSE CROSBY
Villa Robermond
Vence
A.M. [France]
[?March 1930]

Dear Caresse,

I do hope you are better—I came to see you in Paris & you were in London—No wonder you were ill—I rang you up in London & could'nt get at you, then was so busy—Now I am back again & o dear how I miss Lorenzo, in spite of illness & all, his generosity & the life he gave me—I would have loved to have seen you & talked to you, I loved Harry too— When you have time send me the "escaped cock" & the little drawings, it was the last thing he did—If you want some other unpublished thing of his let me know—Hoping to see you some day—Barby my daughter is with me, she also has a slight touch of TB. in the bone, is'nt it too much—She is such a lovely creature—

My love to you, Frieda

XXXIII.
FRIEDA LAWRENCE TO CARESSE CROSBY
Villa Robermond
Vence
A. M. [France]
[?March 1930]

Dear Caresse,

Yes; It was a pity I did'nt see you—I wanted to—Yes, it's difficult to gather up the broken bits of one's life—It was about this time last year that we spent the time with you at the Mill—it's all so vivid to me, that week-end—They were both such vivid creatures, Lorenzo & Harry & I see you in the sailor suit & the bracelet Harry gave you—Barby is a little better, I rushed away from London, could stand no more—I think I can give you something of Lorenzos for a book—But I can't do it yet, because the will is'nt proved, Lawrence died without one; but I'll send you something nice, I hope—I want to go to the ranch and bury Lorenzo there, perhaps you will come one day and see us there. Or here, if ever you come this way. Do send me the little pictures & you will keep the manuscript of the Escaped Cock safe for me, wont you? I hope to goodness I shant have to sell it to live on—You made a beautiful book of it, Lawrence loved it; but I'm not generous enough to give you that Mss alas I cant afford it, either, I fear. But I shall be alright, I think.

Do get better & think how they believed in life & you are so young & must live & gaily—

With much love, I play Harry's gramophone and often think of him & your life together

Frieda

XXXIV.
CARESSE CROSBY TO FRIEDA LAWRENCE
[19 rue de Lille
Paris]
May 26th., 1930

Dear Frieda:—

Your last letter about the manuscript of "THE ESCAPED COCK" has troubled me for some time, because I was sure that Lawrence had given the manuscript to Harry before his death, as he did the manuscript of the "Sun", and I have found, in looking over his letters, a letter to Harry, in which he says that he is sending him the manuscript as a present, because he feels he should have it, being the first one to have brought it out. As I told you, Harry took it to New York with him and I have not got it here in Paris. I enclose the little watercolor motifs, which you asked for.

I am wondering if you are coming through Paris this Spring. I should so like to see you and, as you know, I am awfully anxious to do another one of Lawrence's unpublished stories any time you feel like giving me something.

I love the photograph you sent me. I have a nice one, enlarged from a snapshot, taken here at the Mill, which I am having copied for you and will send you soon.

With ever so many good wishes and most sympathetic thoughts.

Affectionately, Caresse

CC/JC

APPENDIX

The following compilation is a list of Lawrence's letters which contain a significant reference to *The Escaped Cock*. An asterisk denotes those letters which are published in the present volume. The table of abbreviations found below, containing the codes for libraries, other published sources, etc. will assist the reader in locating either the published text or the original manuscript. Also consult the bibliography in Section X of the Commentary, below.

SYMBOLS FOR SOURCES OF PUBLISHED LETTERS

Ald	DHL, *The Selected Letters of D. H. Lawrence*, ed. Richard Aldington.
Brewster	Earl and Achsah Brewster, *D. H. Lawrence: Reminiscences and Correspondence*.
CL	DHL, *The Collected Letters of D. H. Lawrence*, ed. Harry T. Moore.
Cont	Curtis Brown, *Contacts*.
DNR	DHL, "Unterwegs," *Die Neue Rundschau*.
Huxley	DHL, *The Letters of D. H. Lawrence*, ed. Aldous Huxley.
Luhan	Mabel Dodge Luhan, *Lorenzo in Taos*.
NIW	Frieda Lawrence, *Not I But the Wind*.
THsia	"The Unpublished Letters of D. H. Lawrence to Max Mohr," *T'ien Hsia*.
TQ	Maria Chambers, "Afternoons in Italy with D. H. Lawrence."
Trill	DHL, *Selected Letters of D. H. Lawrence*, ed. Diana Trilling.
Zyt	DHL, *The Quest for Rananim*.

SYMBOLS AND ABBREVIATIONS

ALS	Holograph letter signed
MiO	Minor omission in published text
MjO	Major omission in published text
MS	Manuscript
p.	Page
Photostat	The photostatic copy of an unlocated holograph
pp.	Pages
TMS	Typed manuscript
unpub.	Unpublished letter
[ ]	Indication of editorial material
?	Conjectural dating or place of origin

LOCATION OF MANUSCRIPTS

BM	British Museum
CLU	University of California at Los Angeles
CSt	Stanford University
CtY	Yale University
ICarbS	Southern Illinois University
Iowa StEdA	Iowa State Education Association
MH	Harvard University
NBuU	State University of New York at Buffalo
OCU	University of Cincinnati
TxU	University of Texas
Univ Lon	University of London

LETTERS REFERRING TO *THE ESCAPED COCK*

*(1) Monday, 25 April 1927; Villa Mirenda, Florence.
  To CHRISTINE HUGHES. ALS 2 pp. (TxU).

(2) 28 April 1927; Villa Mirenda, Florence.
  To EARL BREWSTER. ALS 1 p. (TxU); Brewster 126 (MiO).

(3) 3 May 1927; Villa Mirenda, Florence.
  To EARL BREWSTER. ALS 4 pp. (TxU); Brewster 126 (MjO), CL 974.

(4) 13 May 1927; Villa Mirenda, Florence.
  To EARL BREWSTER. ALS 2 pp. (TxU); Brewster 129 (MjO), CL 975.

(5) 28 May 1927; Villa Mirenda, Florence.
  To MABEL DODGE LUHAN. MS unlocated; Luhan 329, CL 981.

(6) 8 October 1927; Hotel Eden, Baden-Baden.
  To THE HON. DOROTHY BRETT. ALS 2 pp. (OCU); unpub.

(7) Friday, 21 October 1927; Villa Mirenda, Florence.
  To EARL AND ACHSAH BREWSTER. ALS 2 pp. (TxU); Brewster 150 (MiO), CL 1012.

(8) 18 November 1927; Villa Mirenda, Florence.
  To MABEL DODGE LUHAN. MS unlocated; Luhan 334 (omissions indicated).

*(9) 22 November 1927; Villa Mirenda, Florence.
  To HENRY GODDARD LEACH [Editor of *The Forum*]. ALS 1-1/2 pp. (MH).

*(10) 6 March 1928; Châlet Beau Site, Les Diablerets.
  To THE HON. DOROTHY BRETT. ALS 4 pp. (OCU).

(11) 15 March 1928; Villa Mirenda, Florence.
  To CURTIS BROWN. MS unlocated; Huxley 709, Cont 83.

(12) Tuesday, 16 [17] April 1928; Villa Mirenda, Florence.
  To MARIA HUXLEY. MS unlocated; Huxley 723; Ald 169.

(13) 17 April 1928; Villa Mirenda, Florence.
  To HELEN W. BRAMBLE [Editor of *The Forum*]. MS unlocated; Huxley 726, Trill 279, CL 1057.

(14) 25 April 1928; Villa Mirenda, Florence.
  To THE HON. DOROTHY BRETT. ALS 2 pp. (OCU); Huxley 727 (MjO).

*(15) 3 June 1928; Villa Mirenda, Florence.
  To WILLARD JOHNSON. ALS 2 pp. (CtY).
(16) 21 June 1928; Grand Hotel, Chexbres-sur-Vevey.
  To HARRY CROSBY. ALS 1 p. (ICarbS); unpub.
(17) Sunday morning [? 24 June 1928]; Grand Hotel, Chexbres-sur-Vevey.
  To FRIEDA LAWRENCE. ALS 2 pp. (TxU); NIW 210.
*(18) 20 July 1928; Kesselmatte, Gsteig bei Gstaad.
  To THE HON. DOROTHY BRETT. ALS 2 pp. (OCU).
(19) 27 August 1928; Kesselmatte, Gsteig bei Gstaad.
  To LAURENCE POLLINGER. MS unlocated; Huxley 748, CL 1081.
*(20) Tuesday [? 28 August 1928]; Kesselmatte, Gsteig bei Gstaad.
  To ENID HILTON. ALS 2 pp. (CLU).
(21) 2 September 1928; Kesselmatte, Gsteig bei Gstaad.
  To ENID HILTON. ALS 1 p. (CLU); Huxley 750.
(22) 22 September 1928; Hotel Löwen, Lichtenthal.
  To ENID HILTON. ALS 1-1/2 pp. (CLU); Huxley 753.
*(23) 26 September 1928; Hotel Löwen, Lichtenthal.
  To MARIA CRISTINA CHAMBERS. ALS 2 pp. (CSt).
(24) Saturday [? 27 October 1928]; La Vigie, Ile de Port-Cros.
  To GIUSEPPE ORIOLI. ALS 2 pp. (CLU); unpub.
(25) 7 January 1929; Hotel Beau Rivage, Bandol.
  To CURTIS BROWN. MS unlocated; Huxley 778.
(26) 7 January 1929; Hotel Beau Rivage, Bandol.
  To LAURENCE POLLINGER. MS unlocated; Huxley 778, CL 1114.
*(27) Saturday, 2 March 1929; Hotel Beau Rivage, Bandol.
  To GIUSEPPE ORIOLI. ALS 2 pp. (CLU).
(28) 3 April 1929; Hotel de Versailles, Paris.
  To LAURENCE POLLINGER. MS unlocated; Huxley 791 (omissions indicated).
*(29) 4 April 1929; Hotel de Versailles, Paris.
  To HARRY AND CARESSE CROSBY. ALS 2 pp. (ICarbS).
*(30) 18 April 1929; Hotel Royal, Palma de Mallorca.
  To HARRY AND CARESSE CROSBY. ALS 2 pp. (ICarbS).
*(31) 17 May 1929; Hotel Principe Alfonso, Palma de Mallorca.
  To CARESSE CROSBY. ALS 2 pp. (TxU).
*(32) 20 May 1929; Hotel Principe Alfonso, Palma de Mallorca.
  To HARRY CROSBY. ALS 2 pp. (Iowa StEdA).
(33) 20 May 1929; Hotel Principe Alfonso, Palma de Mallorca.
  To ENID HILTON. ALS 2 pp. (CLU); Huxley 802.
*(34) 7 June 1929; Hotel Principe Alfonso, Palma de Mallorca.
  To HARRY AND CARESSE CROSBY. ALS 2 pp. (Iowa StEdA).
(35) 23 June 1929; Pensione Giuliani, Forte dei Marmi.
  To HARRY AND CARESSE CROSBY. ALS 1 p. (Iowa StEdA); unpub.
(36) 2 August 1929; Kurhaus Plättig, bei Buhl.
  To HARRY AND CARESSE CROSBY. ALS 2 pp. (TxU); Huxley 813.
*(37) 8 August 1929; Hotel Goldner Löwen, Lichtenthal.
  To CHARLES LAHR. TMS (Univ Lon).
(38) Thursday [? 8 August 1929]; Hotel Goldner Löwen, Lichtenthal.
  To CARESSE CROSBY. ALS 2 pp. (TxU); Huxley 755, (MiO), CL 1180.

*(39) 12 August 1929; Hotel Goldner Löwen, Lichtenthal.
To CARESSE CROSBY. ALS 2-1/2 pp. (ICarbS).
*(40) 15 August 1929; Hotel Goldner Löwen, Lichtenthal.
To CARESSE CROSBY. ALS 3 pp. (ICarbS).
*(41) 16 August 1929; Hotel Goldner Löwen, Lichtenthal.
To EDWARD TITUS. ALS 3-1/2 pp. (TxU).
*(42) 9 September 1929; Kaffe Angermaier, Rottach-am-Tegernsee.
To CARESSE CROSBY. ALS 1-1/2 pp. (ICarbS).
*(43) 16 September 1929; Kaffe Angermaier, Rottach-am-Tegernsee.
TO CARESSE CROSBY. ALS 4 pp. (ICarbS).
 (44) 28 September 1929; [as if from] Villa Beau Soleil, Bandol.
To MARIA CRISTINA CHAMBERS. ALS 2 pp. (CSt); CL 1201.
*(45) 28 September 1929; [as if from] Villa Beau Soleil, Bandol.
To CHARLES LAHR. TMS (Univ Lon).
*(46) 28 September 1929; [as if from] Villa Beau Soleil, Bandol.
To CARESSE CROSBY. ALS 1-1/2 pp. (ICarbS).
*(47) 28 September 1929; [as if from] Villa Beau Soleil, Bandol.
To HARRY MARKS. ALS 1 p. (ICarbS).
 (48) 29 September 1929; Hotel Beau Rivage, Bandol.
To LAURENCE POLLINGER. MS unlocated; Huxley 828, CL 1203.
 (49) 7 October 1929; Villa Beau Soleil, Bandol.
To CHARLES LAHR. ALS 2 pp. (NBuU); CL 1206.
*(50) 11 October 1929; Villa Beau Soleil, Bandol.
To MARIA CRISTINA CHAMBERS. ALS 2 pp. (CSt).
 (51) 11 October 1929; Villa Beau Soleil, Bandol.
To CHARLES LAHR. ALS 2 pp. (NBuU); unpub.
*(52) 15 October 1929; Villa Beau Soleil, Bandol.
To CARESSE CROSBY. ALS 2 pp. (TxU).
 (53) 23 October 1929; Villa Beau Soleil, Bandol.
To CARESSE CROSBY. ALS 1 p. (ICarbS); unpub.
 (54) 25 October 1929; Villa Beau Soleil, Bandol.
To MARIA CRISTINA CHAMBERS. ALS 1 p. (CSt); unpub.
 (55) 1 November 1929; Villa Beau Soleil, Bandol.
To CARESSE CROSBY. ALS 1-1/2 pp. (ICarbS); Huxley 837.
 (56) 1 November 1929; Villa Beau Soleil, Bandol.
To GIUSEPPE ORIOLI. ALS 1 p. (CLU); unpub.
 (57) 2 November 1929; Villa Beau Soleil, Bandol.
To MARIA CRISTINA CHAMBERS. ALS 2 pp. (TxU); unpub.
(part of MS obliterated).
 (58) 2 November 1929; Villa Beau Soleil, Bandol.
To CHARLES LAHR. ALS 1 p. (NBuU); unpub.
 (59) 9 November 1929; Villa Beau Soleil, Bandol.
To GIUSEPPE ORIOLI. ALS 2 pp. (CLU); unpub.
 (60) Saturday [? 9 November 1929]; Villa Beau Soleil, Bandol.
To CARESSE CROSBY. ALS 1 p. (ICarbS); unpub.
*(61) Saturday [? 9 November 1929]; Villa Beau Soleil, Bandol.
To CHARLES LAHR. TMS (Univ Lon).
 (62) Wednesday [? 20 November 1929]; Villa Beau Soleil, Bandol.
To CHARLES LAHR. ALS 2 pp. (NBuU); unpub.

(63) Wednesday [? 20 November 1929]; Villa Beau Soleil, Bandol.
    To GIUSEPPE ORIOLI. ALS 2 pp. (CLU); CL 1214.

(64) Wednesday [? 27 November 1929]; Villa Beau Soleil, Bandol.
    To S. S. KOTELIANSKY. ALS 1-1/2 pp. (BM); CL 1217; Zyt 392.

(65) Wednesday [? 11 December 1929]; Villa Beau Soleil, Bandol.
    To EDWARD TITUS. ALS 1 p. (TxU); unpub.

(66) 19 December 1929; Villa Beau Soleil, Bandol.
    To MAX AND KATHE MOHR. MS unlocated; THsia, September, 177; DNR II 538 [Ger].

(67) 23 December 1929; Villa Beau Soleil, Bandol.
    To CHARLES LAHR. ALS 1 p. (NBuU); unpub.

(68) 20 January 1930; Villa Beau Soleil, Bandol.
    To CARESSE CROSBY. ALS 2 pp. [Photostat (ICarbS)]; Huxley 847, Trill 307, CL 1234.

(69) 21 January 1930; Villa Beau Soleil, Bandol.
    To MARIA CRISTINA CHAMBERS. TMS (TxU); TQ 119 (MjO).

*(70) 24 January 1930; Villa Beau Soleil, Bandol.
    To CHARLES LAHR. ALS 1 p. (NBuU).

(71) 3 February 1930; Villa Beau Soleil, Bandol.
    To CHARLES LAHR. ALS 2 pp. (NBuU); CL 1239.

*(72) 9 February 1930; Ad Astra, Vence.
    To CHARLES LAHR. ALS 1 p. (NBuU).

(73) 14 February 1930; Ad Astra, Vence.
    To CARESSE CROSBY. ALS 2 pp. (TxU); CL 1243.

*(74) 20 February 1930; Ad Astra, Vence.
    To CHARLES LAHR. ALS 1 p. (Univ Lon).

(75) 20 February 1930; Ad Astra, Vence.
    To LAURENCE POLLINGER. MS unlocated; Huxley 852, CL 1244.

"The Escaped Cock"
Original Short Story Version of Part I
reprinted from
The Forum, February 1928

There was a peasant near Jerusalem who acquired a young gamecock which looked a shabby little thing, but which put on brave feathers as spring advanced and was resplendent with an arched and orange neck by the time the fig trees were letting out leaves from their end tips.

This peasant was poor. He lived in a cottage of mud brick and had only a little, dirty, inner courtyard with a tough fig tree for all his territory. He worked hard among the vines and olives and wheat of his master, then came home to sleep in the mud brick cottage by the path. But he was rather proud of his young rooster. In the shut-in yard were three shabby hens which laid small eggs, shed the few feathers they had, and made a disproportionate amount of dirt. There was also, in a corner under the straw roof, a dull donkey that often went with the peasant to work but sometimes stayed at home. And there was the peasant's wife, a black-browed, youngish woman who did not work too hard. She threw a little grain or the remains of the porridge mess to the fowls and she cut green fodder with a sickle for the ass.

The young cock grew to a certain splendor. By some freak of destiny he was a dandy rooster, in that dirty little yard with three patchy hens. He learned to crane his neck and give shrill answers to the crowing of other cocks beyond the walls, in a world he knew nothing of. But there was a special fiery clamor to his crow, and the distant calling of other cocks roused him to unexpected outbursts.

"How he sings!" said the peasant, as he got up and pulled his day-shirt over his head.

"He is good for twenty hens," said the wife.

The peasant went out and looked with pride at his young rooster. A saucy, flamboyant bird that had already made the final acquaintance of the three tattered hens. But the cockerel was tipping his head, listening to the challenge of far-off, unseen cocks in the unknown world. Ghost voices, crowing at him mysteriously out of limbo. He answered with a ringing defiance, never to be daunted.

"He will surely fly away, one of these days," said the peasant's wife.

103

So they lured him with grain, caught him though he fought with all his wings and feet, and they tied a cord round his shank, fastening it against the spur, and they tied the other end of the cord to the post that held up the donkey's straw pent-roof.

The young cock, freed, marched with a prancing stride of indignation away from the humans, came to the end of his string, gave a tug and a hitch of his tied leg, fell over for a moment, scuffled frantically on the unclean, earthen floor, to the horror of the shabby hens, then, with a sickening lurch, regained his feet and stood to think. The peasant and the peasant's wife laughed heartily, and the young cock heard them. And he knew, with a gloomy, foreboding kind of knowledge, that he was tied by the leg.

He no longer pranced and ruffled and forged his feathers. He walked within the limits of his tether sombrely. Still he gobbled up the best bits of food. Still, sometimes, he saved an extra-best bit for his favorite hen of the moment. Still he pranced with quivering, rocking fierceness upon such of his harem as came nonchalantly within range and gave off the invisible lure. And still he crowed defiance to the cockcrows that showered up out of limbo, in the dawn.

But there was now a grim voracity in the way he gobbled his food and a pinched triumph in the way he seized upon the shabby hens. His voice, above all, had lost the full gold of its clangor. He was tied by the leg and he knew it. Body, soul, and spirit were tied by that string.

Underneath, however, the life in him was grimly unbroken. It was the cord that should break. So one morning, just before the light of dawn, rousing from his slumbers with a sudden wave of strength, he leaped forward on his wings and the string snapped. He gave a wild, strange squawk, rose in one lift to the top of the wall, and there he crowed a loud and splitting crow. So loud, it woke the peasant.

At the same time, at the same hour before dawn, the same morning, a man awoke from a long sleep in which he was tied up. He woke numb and cold, inside a carved hole in the rock. Through all the long, long sleep his body had been full of hurt and it was still full of hurt. He did not open his eyes. Yet he knew he was awake, and numb, and cold, and rigid, and full of hurt, and tied up. His face was banded with cold bands, his legs were bandaged together. Only his hands were loose.

He could move if he wanted: he knew that. But he had no want. Who would want him to come back from the dead? A deep, deep nausea stirred in him, at the premonition of movement. He resented already the fact of the strange, incalculable moving that had already taken place in him: the moving back into consciousness. He had not wished it. He had wanted to stay outside, in the place where even memory is stone dead.

104

But now, something had returned him, like a returned letter, and in the return he lay overcome with a sense of nausea. Yet suddenly his hands moved. They lifted up, cold, heavy, and sore. Yet they lifted up, to drag away the cloth from his face and to push at the shoulder bands. Then they fell again, cold, heavy, numb, and sick with having moved even so much, unspeakably unwilling to move farther.

With his face cleared and his shoulders free, he lapsed again and lay dead, resting on the cold nullity of being dead. It was the most desirable. And almost, he had it complete: the utter cold nullity of being outside.

Yet when he was most nearly gone, suddenly, driven by an ache at the wrists, his hands rose and began pushing at the bandages of his knees, his feet began to stir, even while his breast lay cold and dead still.

And at last the eyes opened. On to the dark. The same dark! Yet perhaps there was a pale chink of the all-disturbing light, prizing open the pure dark. He could not lift his head. The eyes closed. And again it was finished.

Then suddenly he leaned up, and the great world reeled. Bandages fell away. And narrow walls of rock closed upon him, and gave the new anguish of imprisonment. There were chinks of light. With a wave of strength that came from revulsion, he leaned forward in that narrow cell of rock and leaned frail hands on the rock near the chinks of light.

Strength came from somewhere, from revulsion, there was a crash and a wave of light, and the dead man was crouching in his lair, facing the elemental onrush of light. Yet it was hardly dawn. And the strange, piercing keenness of daybreak's sharp breath was on him. It meant full awakening.

Slowly, slowly he crept down from the cell of rock, with the caution of the bitterly wounded. Bandages and linen and perfume fell away, and he crouched on the ground against the wall of rock, to recover oblivion. But he saw his hurt feet touching the earth again, with unspeakable pain, the earth they had meant to touch no more; and he saw his thin legs that had died; and pain unknowable, pain like utter bodily disillusion, filled him so full that he stood up, with one torn hand on the ledge of the tomb.

To be back! To be back again, after all that! He saw the linen swathing bands fallen round his dead feet and stooping, he picked them up, folded them, and laid them back in the rocky cavity from which he had emerged. Then he took the perfumed linen sheet, wrapped it round him as a mantle, and turned away, to the wanness of the chill dawn. He was alone; and having died, was even beyond loneliness.

Filled still with the sickness of unspeakable disillusion, the man stepped with wincing feet down the rocky slope, past the sleeping soldiers, who lay wrapped in their woolen mantles under the wild laurels. Silent, on naked, scarred feet, wrapped in a white linen shroud, he glanced down for a moment on the inert, heap-like bodies of the soldiers. They were repulsive, a slow squalor of limbs, yet he felt a certain compassion. He passed on toward the road lest they should wake.

Having nowhere to go, he turned away from the city that stood on her hills. He slowly followed the road away from the town, past the olives, under which purple anemones were drooping in the chill of dawn, and rich green herbage was pressing thick. The world, the same as ever, the natural world, thronging with greenness, a nightingale winsomely, wistfully, coaxingly calling from the bushes beside a runnel of water, in the world, the natural world of morning and evening, forever undying, from which he had died.

He went on, on scarred feet, neither of this world nor of the next. Neither here nor there, neither seeing nor yet sightless, he passed dimly on, away from the city and its precincts, wondering why he should be traveling, yet driven by a dim, deep nausea of disillusion and a resolution of which he was not even aware.

Advancing in a kind of half-consciousness under the dry-stone wall of the olive orchard, he was roused by the shrill, wild crowing of a cock just near him, a sound which made him shiver as if electricity had touched him. He saw a black and orange cock on a bough above the road, then running through the olives of the upper level, a peasant in a gray, woolen shirt-tunic. Leaping out of greenness came the black and orange cock with the red comb, his tail feathers streaming lustrous.

"Oh, stop him, Master!" called the peasant. "My escaped cock!"

The man addressed, with a sudden flicker of smile, opened his great, white wings of a shroud in front of the leaping bird. The cock fell back with a squawk and a flutter, the peasant jumped forward, there was a terrific beating of wings and whirring of feathers, then the peasant had the escaped cock safely under his arm, its wings shut down, its face crazily craning forward, its round eye goggling from its white chops.

"It's my escaped cock!" said the peasant, soothing the bird with his left hand, as he looked perspiringly up into the face of the man wrapped in white linen.

The peasant changed countenance and stood transfixed, as he looked into the dead-white face of the man who had died. That dead-white face, so still, with the black beard growing on it as if in death; and those wide open, black, sombre eyes that had died; and those washed scars on the waxy forehead! The slow-blooded man of the fields let his jaw drop in childish inability to meet the situation.

"Don't be afraid," said the man in the shroud. "I am not dead. They took me down too soon. So I have risen up. Yet if they discover me, they will do it all over again. . . ."

He spoke in a voice of old disgust. Humanity! Especially humanity in authority! There was only one thing it could do. He looked with black, indifferent eyes into the quick, shifty eyes of the peasant. The peasant quailed and was powerless under the look of deathly indifference and strange, cold resoluteness. He could only say the one thing he was really afraid to say:

"Will you hide in my house, Master?"

"I will rest there. But if you tell anyone, you know what will happen. You, too, will have to go before a judge."

"Me! I shan't speak! Let us be quick!"

The peasant looked round in fear, wondering sulkily why he had let himself in for this doom. The man with scarred feet climbed painfully up to the level of the olive garden and followed the sullen, hurrying peasant across the green wheat among the olive trees. He felt the cool silkiness of the young wheat under his feet that had been dead, and the roughishness of its separate life was apparent to him. At the edges of rocks he saw the silky, silvery-haired buds of the scarlet anemone bending downward, and they too were in another world. In his own world he was alone, utterly alone. These things around him were in a world that had never died. But he himself had died or had been killed from out of it, and all that remained now was the great, void nausea of utter disillusion.

They came to a clay cottage, and the peasant waited dejectedly for the other man to pass.

"Pass!" he said. "Pass! We have not been seen."

The man in white linen entered the earthen room, taking with him the aroma of strange perfumes. The peasant closed the door and passed through the inner doorway to the yard, where the ass stood within the high walls, safe from being stolen. There the peasant, in great disquietude, tied up the cock. The man with the waxen face sat down on a mat near the hearth, for he was spent and barely conscious. Yet he heard outside the whispering of the peasant to his wife, for the woman had been watching from the roof.

Presently they came in, and the woman hid her face. She poured water, and put bread and dried figs on a wooden platter.

"Eat, Master!" said the peasant. "No one has seen. Eat!"

But the stranger had no desire for food. Yet he moistened a little bread in the water, and ate it, since life must be. But desire was dead in him, even for food and drink. He had risen without desire, without even the desire to live, empty save for the all-overwhelming disillusion

107

that lay like nausea where his life had been. Yet perhaps, deeper even than disillusion, was a desireless resoluteness, deeper even than consciousness.

The peasant and his wife stood near the door, watching. They saw with terror the livid wounds on the thin, waxy hands and the thin feet of the stranger, and the small lacerations in his still-dead forehead. They smelled with terror the scent of rich perfumes that came from him, from his body. And they looked at the fine, snowy, costly linen. Perhaps really he was a dead king, from the region of terrors. And he was still cold and remote in the region of death, with perfumes coming from his transparent body as if from some strange flower.

Having with difficulty swallowed some of the moistened bread, he lifted his eyes to them. He saw them as they were: limited, meagre in their life, without any splendor of gesture and of courage. But they were what they were, slow, inevitable parts of the natural world. They had no nobility, but fear made them compassionate.

And the stranger had compassion on them again, for he knew that they would respond best to gentleness, giving back a clumsy gentleness again.

"Do not be afraid," he said to them gently. "Let me stay a little while with you. I shall not stay long. And then I shall go away forever. But do not be afraid. No harm will come to you through me."

They believed him at once, yet the fear did not leave them. And they said:

"Stay, Master, while ever you will. Rest! Rest quietly!"

But they were afraid.

So he let them be, and the peasant went away with the ass. The sun had risen bright, and in the dark house with the door shut the man was again as if in the tomb. So he said to the woman: "I would lie in the yard." And she swept the yard for him and laid him a mat, and he lay down under the wall in the morning sun. There he saw the first green leaves spurting like flames from the ends of the enclosed fig tree, out of the bareness to the sky of spring above. But the man who had died could not look, he only lay quite still in the sun which was not yet too hot, and had no desire in him, not even to move. But he lay with his thin legs in the sun, his black, perfumed hair falling into the hollows of his neck, and his thin, colorless arms utterly inert. As he lay there the hens clucked and scratched, and the escaped cock, caught and tied by the leg again, cowered in a corner.

The peasant woman was frightened. She came peeping and, seeing him never move, feared to have a dead man in the yard. But the sun had grown stronger. He opened his eyes and looked at her. And now she was frightened of the man who was alive, but spoke nothing.

He opened his eyes, and saw the world again bright as glass. It was life, in which he had no share any more. But it shone outside him, blue sky, and a bare fig tree with little jets of green leaf. Bright as glass, and he was not of it, for desire had failed.

Yet he was there and not extinguished. The day passed in a kind of coma, and at evening he went into the house. The peasant man came home, but he was frightened and had nothing to say. The stranger, too, ate of the mess of beans, a little. Then he washed his hands and turned to the wall and was silent. The peasants were silent too. They watched their guest sleep. Sleep was so near death, he could still sleep.

Yet when the sun came up, he went again to lie in the yard. The sun was the one thing that drew him and swayed him, and he still wanted to feel the cool air of morning in his nostrils and the pale sky overhead. He still hated to be shut up.

As he came out, the young cock crowed. It was a diminished, pinched cry, but there was that in the voice of the bird stronger than chagrin. It was the assertion of life, the loud outcry of the cock's petty triumph in life. The man who had died stood and watched the cock who had escaped and been caught ruffling himself up, rising forward on his toes, throwing out his chest and parting his beak in another challenge to all the world to deny his existence. "Deny my existence if you can!" the brave sounds rang out, and though they were diminished by the cord round the bird's leg, they were effective enough.

The man who had died looked grimly on life and saw a vast assertiveness everywhere flinging itself up in stormy or subtle wave-crests, foam-tips emerging out of the blue invisible, a black and orange cock, or the green flame tongues out of the extremes of the fig tree. They came forth, these things and creatures of spring, raging with insistence and with assertion. They came brandishing themselves like crests of foam out of the blue flood of the invisible, out of the vast invisible sea of strength, and they came colored and tangible, evanescent, yet deathless in their coming. The man who had died looked on the great, violent swing into existence of things that had not died, but he saw no longer their tremulous desire to exist and to be. He heard instead their ringing, defiant challenge to all other things existing, their raging assertion of themselves.

The man lay still, with eyes that had died now wide open and darkly still, seeing the everlasting, self-assertive violence of life. And the cock, with a flat, brilliant glance, glanced back at him with a bird's half-seeing look, suspicious. And always the man who had died saw not the bird alone, but the short, snappy wave of life of which the bird was the crest.

109

He watched the queer, beaky motion of the creature as it gobbled into itself the scraps of food, its glancing of the eye of life, ever alert and watchful, overweening and cautious, and the voice of its life, crowing triumph and assertion, yet strangled by a cord of circumstance. He seemed to hear the queer speech of very life, as the cock triumphantly imitated the cackling of the favorite hen when she had laid an egg, a cackling which still had, in the male bird, the hollow chagrin of the cord round his leg. And when the man threw a bit of bread to the cock, it called with an extraordinary cooing tenderness, tousling and saving the morsel for the hens. The hens ran up greedily, and carried the morsel away beyond the reach of the string.

Then, walking complacently after them, suddenly the male bird's leg would hitch at the end of his tether and he would yield with a kind of collapse. His flag fell, he seemed to diminish, he would huddle in the shade. And he was young, his tail feathers, glossy as they were, were not fully grown.

It was not till evening again that the tide of life in him made him forget. Then when his favorite hen came strolling unconcernedly near him, emitting the lure, he pounced on her with all his feathers vibrating. And the man who had died watched the unsteady, rocking vibration of the bent bird, and it was not the bird he saw, but one wave-tip of life overlapping for a minute another, in the tide of the raging ocean of life. And the rage of life seemed more fierce and compulsive to him even than the rage of death. The scythe-stroke of death was a shadow, compared to the raging upstarting of life, the determined turmoil of life. And this mad insistence of chaotic life, everything insisting against everything else, was repellent to the man who had died. He looked on, relieved that it was no longer his affair.

At twilight the peasant came home with the ass and he said:

"Master! It is said the body was stolen from the garden and the tomb is empty, and the soldiers are taken away, accursed Romans! And the women are there to weep."

The man who had died looked at the man who had not died.

"It is well," he said. "Say nothing, and we are safe."

And the peasant was relieved. He looked rather dirty and stupid, and even as much flaminess as that of the young cock which he had tied by the leg, would never glow in him. He was without fire. But the man who had died thought to himself: "Why then should he be lifted up? Clods of earth are turned over for refreshment, they are not to be lifted up. Let the earth remain earthy and hold its own against the sky. I was wrong to seek to lift it up. It was wrong to try to interfere. The plowshare of devastation will be set in the soil of Judaea, and the life of this peasant will be overturned like the sods of the field. No man can save the earth from tillage. It is tillage, not salvation. . . ."

So he saw the man, the peasant, without emotion; for the man who had died no longer wished to interfere in the fate of the man who had not died and who, when he did die, would return to earth. Let him return to earth in his own good hour, and let no one try to interfere when the earth claims her own.

So the man with scars let the peasant go from him, for the peasant had his own destiny as a clod of earth with a little fire in it. Yet the man who had died said to himself: "He is my host."

And at dawn, when he was better, the man who had died rose up, and on slow, sore feet retraced his way to the garden. For he had been betrayed in a garden and buried in a garden. And as he turned round the screen of laurel near the rock-face, he saw a woman hovering close to the tomb, a woman in blue and yellow. She peeped again into the mouth of the hole, that was like a deep cupboard. But still there was nothing. And she wrung her hands and wept. And as she turned away, she saw the man in white standing by the laurels, and she gave a cry, thinking it might be a spy, and she said:

"They have taken him away!"

So he said to her:

"Madeleine!"

Then she stood as if she would fall, for she knew him. And he said to her:

"Madeleine! Do not be afraid. I am alive. They took me down too soon, so I came back to life. Then I was sheltered in a house."

She did not know what to say but wished to fall at his feet. He prevented her, saying:

"Don't touch me, Madeleine. I am not yet healed and in touch with men."

So she wept, because she did not know what to do. And he said:

"Let us go aside among the bushes where we can speak unseen."

So in her blue mantle and her yellow robe, she followed him among the trees, and he sat down under a myrtle bush. And he said:

"I am not yet quite come to. Madeleine, what is to be done next?"

"Master!" she said. "Oh, we have wept for you! And will you come back to us?"

"For me, all that is finished, I have been taken away from it," he said. "The stream will run till there are no more rains, then it will dry up. For me, those heavens are no more over me."

"And will you give up your triumph?" she asked sadly.

"My triumph?" he asked. "But what was my triumph? I was killed

111

in my mission and it is dead now to me. I can't come back. I am in another world, Madeleine, and not in touch with men. Yet still I am a man and still young. Is it not so? What will be the outcome, since now I am dead and risen, there is a gulf between me and all mankind? I am out of touch."

She heard him, and did not understand. Only she felt a heavy disappointment rise up in her.

"But you will come back to us?" she humbly insisted.

"I cannot know what I shall do," he said. "When I am healed, perhaps I shall know. But my mission is over, death has utterly cut it off from me. When a man dies, he rises in another world, even if there are the same faces. Death has put me far beyond even that salvation I dreamed of. Oh, Madeleine, I don't know what world I have risen to. But I have risen out of touch with the old. And now I wait for my Father to take me up again."

Madeleine heard the estrangement in his voice, and her heart was cold and angry.

"Do you betray us all?" she said.

"Betray?" he said. "Death has betrayed me. I am different. My poor Judas, he handed death to me. He rescued me from my own salvation. No man can know his own salvation. Death makes all things different. Now Judas and I alone understand."

Madeleine heard without understanding, but she pondered bitterly. "You want to be alone henceforward?" she said. "Have you risen for yourself alone?"

He heard the reproach in her voice, and looked at her beautiful face, which still was dense with insistence. She had been so happy to be saved from her old rapacity and to devote herself to a pure Messiah. But now she had this doom upon her, instead of the old one: she was now greedy to give her selfless devotion, as before she had been greedy to take from her lovers. But the man who had died felt her insistent, selfless devotion clutching his body with a new, bodiless greed, and the nausea of old pain filled him.

"A man would not die the same death twice," he said to her.

She glanced up at him, and saw the weariness settling again on his waxy face and the vast disillusion in his dark eyes and the underlying indifference to all things. There was revulsion in her glance, which he felt. And he said to himself: "Now my own followers will want to do me to death again, because I have risen up from the dead different from their expectation."

"But you will come to us, to see us, us who love you?" she said.

He laughed a little, and said:

112

"Ah, yes!" Then he added: "Have you a little money? Will you give me a little money? I owe it."

She had not much, but it pleased her to give it him.

"Do you think," he said to her, "that I might come and live with you in your house?"

She looked up at him with large, blue eyes that gleamed strangely.

"Now?" she said, with peculiar triumph.

And he, who shrank now from triumph of any sort, his own or another's, said:

"Not now! Later, when I am healed, and I am with my Father." The words faltered in him, and in his heart, he knew he would never go to live in her house. For the flicker of triumph had gleamed in her eyes; the greed of giving. But she murmured, in a humming rapture:

"Ah, you know I would give up everything to you."

"Nay!" he said. "I didn't ask that."

A revulsion from all the life he had known came over him again, the great nausea of disillusion, and the spear-thrust through his bowels. He crouched under the myrtle bushes, without strength. Yet his eyes were open. And she looked at him again, and she saw that it was not the Messiah. The Messiah had not risen. The enthusiasm and the burning purity was gone, and the rapt youth. His youth was dead. This man was middle-aged and disillusioned, with a certain terrible indifference and a resoluteness which love would never conquer. This was not the Master she had so adored, the young, flamy, unphysical exalter of her soul. This was nearer to the lovers she had known of old, but with a greater indifference to the personal issue and a lesser susceptibility.

She was thrown out of the balance of her rapturous, anguished adoration. This risen man was the death of her dream.

"You should go now," he said to her. "Do not touch me, I am in death. I shall come again here, on the third day. Come if you will, at dawn. And we will speak again."

She went away, perturbed and shattered. Yet as she went, her mind discarded the bitterness of the reality, and she conjured up rapture and wonder that the Master was risen and was not dead. He was risen, the Savior, the exalter, the wonder-worker! He was risen, but not as man— as pure God, who should not be touched by flesh and who should be rapt away into heaven. It was the most glorious and most ghostly of the miracles.

Meanwhile, the man who had died gathered himself together at last and slowly made his way to the peasant's house. He was glad to go back to them and away from Madeleine and his own associates. For the peasants had the inertia of earth and would let him rest, and as yet, would put no compulsion on him.

The woman was on the roof, looking for him. She was afraid that he had gone away. His presence in the house had cast a certain spell over her, like mountains that gleam in the distance. It was the living remoteness. She hastened to the door, to him.

"Where have you been, Master?" she said shyly. "Why did you go away?"

"I have been to walk in a garden, and I have seen a friend who gave me a little money. It is for you."

He held out his thin hand with the small amount of money, all that Madeleine could give him. The peasant wife's eyes glistened, for money was scarce, and she said:

"Oh, Master! And is it truly mine?"

"Take it!" he said. "It is due to you."

So he lay down in the yard again, sick with relief at being alone again. For with the peasants he could be alone, but his own friends would never let him be alone. And in the safety of the yard the young cock was dear to him as it crowed in the helpless zest of life, then finished in the helpless humiliation of being tied by the leg. This day the ass stood swishing her tail under the shed. The man who had died lay down and turned utterly away from life, in the sickness of death in life.

But the woman brought wine and water and sweetened cakes, and roused him, so that he ate a little, to please her. The day was hot, with a fierceness after a shower of rain, and as she crouched to serve him, he saw her breasts sway from her humble body under her smock. He knew she wished he would desire her, and she was youngish and not uncomely. And he, who had never known a woman, would have desired her if he could. But he could not want her, though he felt gently toward her soft, humble, crouching body. But his own body kept aloof. Perhaps it was her thoughts, her consciousness, he could not mingle with. He had given her money, and she was pleased, so now she thought he would want this other of her. But her little soul was shortsighted and hard; she could never make the inner gift of her body. What was worth having would never be given.

So he spoke a little, quiet word to her and turned away. He could not touch the little, personal body—the little, personal life—in this woman nor in any other. He turned away and abided by the greater ruling.

Having died and risen, he realized at last that the body, too, has its purity and its impurity, its little and its greater life. Out of fear of the impurity, he had remained virgin, in his little life of fear. But now he realized that virginity, too, is a form of greed. He turned away even from himself. And he lay as if dead.

114

He had risen bodily from the dead, but what his body had come alive for he did not know. He only knew that was bodily out of touch with mankind; he who had previously *held* himself out of touch, in his little life, now was beyond touch. He had no desire in him, save the desire that none should touch him.

The peasant came home from work and said:

"Master, I thank you for the money. And all I have is yours."

And the man who died saw the peasant stand there with bright, excited eyes, animated by the hope of greater sums of money later on. And he wondered again over the little body of man, and the little life of man, so rarely suffused with the greater glow. How was it the peasant did not feel the absence of the other glow in him?

And the peasant looked at the man who had died and saw his frailty and the death still in his body, and the peasant was afraid and hugged his own health. Yet the remoteness of the man who had died had a wonder and a sort of fascination for the man who had not died. So the night having fallen, he would have helped the frail man to rise. But the other said to him:

"No, don't touch me. I am sore."

The sun rose ever again, in the rage of life, and burnished the young cock brighter. But the peasant kept the string renewed, and the bird was a prisoner. The flame of life nevertheless mounted to a sharper brightness in the creature, so that it eyed askance and haughtily the man who had died. And the man smiled, and said to it: "Surely thou forgettest even the string, thou father among birds!" And the young cock, answering, crowed.

When at dawn on the third morning the man went to the garden, he was absorbed, thinking how the body could live a greater life, how this should come to pass. For he was beyond touch of the little, personal bodies of people. So he came suddenly through the thick screen of laurel and myrtle bushes, near the rock, suddenly, and he saw three women near the tomb. One was Madeleine, and one was the woman who had been his mother, and the third was a woman he knew, called Joan.

He looked up and saw them all, and they saw him, and they were all afraid. He stood arrested in the distance, knowing they were there to claim him back, bodily. But he would in no wise return to them. Pallid, in the shadow of a gray morning that was blowing to rain, he saw them and turned away. But Madeleine hastened toward him.

"I did not bring them," she said. "They have come of themselves. See, I have brought you money! Will you not come and speak to them?" She offered him some gold pieces, and he took them saying:

"May I have this money? I shall need it. I can not speak to them. I am not yet risen to the Father. And now I must go away."

"Ah! Where will you go?" she cried.

He looked at her and felt her clutching at him for the man who was dead in him, the man of his little life, of his youth and his mission, of his chastity and his fear and his doctrine of salvation.

"I must go to my Father," he said.

"And will you leave us? There is your mother!" she cried, turning round with the old anguish which yet was sweet to her.

"But now I must ascend to my Father," he said, and he drew back into the bushes and so turned quickly and went away, saying to himself: "Now I belong to my Father, though I know not what he is, nor where he is. And still he is."

So he went back to the peasant's house, to the yard where the young cock was tied by the leg with a string. And he wanted no one, for now he could only be alone; for the presence of people opened his wounds. The sun and the biting salve of spring were healing him, even the gaping wound of disillusion through his bowels was hardening up. But his connection with men and women, his urge to save them or to be saved by them, this had gone from him for good. He wondered what he should do, for it seemed strange to be in a world of men and women and to have no touch with them. He said to himslf: "Why has the connection of touch gone out of me?"

But in the tomb the connection had perished. Therefore he went no more to the garden but lay still while the sun shone, or walked at dusk across the olive slopes, among the green wheat that rose a palm-breadth higher every sunny day. And always he thought to himself: Some things make no clamor and do not insist; they are only dauntless. The iris is naked on the inner air, opens its sharp buds alone and touches nothing. Only man is afraid to unfurl his nakedness; and when he touches something he becomes greedy, and when something touches him he is afraid. Why can not man stand like an iris within the inner air, naked and all himself, with the Father. The inner air is my Father, and all things blossom within his body.

So he saw the green jets of leaves unspread on the fig tree with the bright, translucent, green blood of the tree. And the young cock grew brighter, more lustrous with the sun's burnishing, yet always tied by the leg with a string. And the sun went down more and more in pomp out of the gold and red-flushed air. The man who had died beheld it all and he thought: "It is fear of death which makes man unclean. He is afraid to unfold his nakedness because of the fear in him, and he is greedy for all he touches because he is afraid he is nothing in himself. I cannot

116

touch my fellow men because they smell of greed and fear. It is fear of death that hampers them. Why don't they die, to be rid of their staleness and their littleness, covered up as they are and gnawed by the weariness of their greed and the compulsion of their fear? But it is vain to speak. Words are like midges that bite at evening and blister men with conceit. Man is tormented with clouds of words like midges, and they follow him right to the tomb. But beyond the tomb they cannot go. Why will man never die and pass the place where words can bite no more? On the other side the air is clear, and there is nothing to insist on. Then a man can be well within his own skin, like an iris on its stem, within the inner air, and he can be naked as a flower is, and fearless as the iris, because it stands within the Father. Now may I stand within the Father."

So he healed of his wounds and enjoyed the immortality of being alive without fret. For in the tomb he had slipped the noose of his little self, which is bound by care. Now his greater self healed and became whole within his skin, and he smiled to himself, having discovered the inner world of insouciance, which is immortality.

Then he said to himself: "I will wander the earth and say nothing; for strange is the phenomenal world, whose essential body is my Father. I will wander like an iris walking naked within the inner air, well within the Father, and I shall be in the outer air as well. I shall see all the noise and the dust, and smell the fear, and brush past the greed, and beware. But I will go with the Father around me, with my body erect and procreant within the inner air. Perhaps within the inner air I shall meet other men, perhaps women, and we shall be in touch. If not, it is no matter, for my movement and my uprising is within the Father, and I stand naked within him as the irises do. And he is all about me, and my whole body is procreant in him."

So he communed with himself and decided to be a physician. Because the power was still in him to heal whomsoever touched him within the Father. Therefore he cut his hair and his beard after the right fashion and smiled to himself. And he bought himself shoes and the right mantle, and put the right cloth over his head, hiding all the little scars. And the peasant said:

"Master, will you go forth from us?"

"Yea, for the time is come for me to return to the Father."

So he gave the peasant a piece of money, and said to him:

"Give me the cock that escaped and is now tied by the leg. For he shall ascend with me."

So for a piece of money the peasant gave the cock to the man who was setting forth, and at dawn the man who had died set out into the phenomenal world, to walk among the outer dust, yet keep himself well within the inner air, which he called the Father. And he said to himself: "I must, perforce touch them casually, though they smell of greed and fear." So a little unwillingly he lifted the hot and feathery body of the cock and carried the bird under his arm, saying: "Better thee than another." And the cock did not fuss but settled down quietly; and his tail fluttered gaily behind, and he craned his head excitedly, for he too was adventuring out for the first time into the phenomenal world, whose inner air is the body of the god of cocks also. The peasant woman shed a few tears but then went indoors, being a peasant, to look again at the pieces of money. And it seemed to her a gleam came out of the pieces of money, wonderful.

The man who had died wandered on, and it was a day of early summer while greenness still flourished under the sun. He went slowly and saw the world in motion, and he stood aside as a pack train went by toward the city. And he said to himself: "Strange is the phenomenal world, dirty and clean together. And I am the same. Nothing is clean but what is also dirty. The outer air is dirty with fear; for all beasts, but especially man, sweat greed and fear till the atmosphere of men stinks. If they would but die, they would be so much cleaner on the air. But it is best to say nothing. Words cake like mud wherever they fall. And man is foul and caked already with the mud of old words. If he would but die and be washed! They killed me for preaching, yet new words are no worse than old. And men will cake themselves up with my words also, till they are heavy with the caked mud thereof. So it is! And if they will not go into the bath, the deluge will fall on them. And some, no doubt, will rise out of the inner earth, which is the Father, like flowers upon the inner air, which is the Father the same. And from the Father under the earth to the Father over the earth, they will unfold their nakedness entire as the irises do that rise from mud, glistening in the inner air. Whereas men and women now are covered up, and they hug their staleness to themselves. They uncover a fragment of their nakedness, and the man penetrates greedily a little way into a woman. But he must draw back, disappointed, disappointing the woman. Men and women are forever a disappointment and a chagrin to one another. They seek what they cannot get. But if a man would wash himself with death, he could stand erect and quite naked, with all his body within the Father. And perhaps within the Father he could meet a woman erect and quite uncovered and encompassed by the Father as the iris is. Then they could put the difference of their nakedness together and not be disappointed. For the great fulfillment is to be with the Father, and the whole body encompassed. But now, men are less adept than the young

118

cock under my arm. I see him at dawn stretch himself within the inner air, and all is well with him. Yet my arm is weary of the weight and heat of him, and I shall be glad to set him down in a kingdom of cocks. I shall go on to that village on the hill ahead of me, for day is declining. It will be pleasant to order food, and sleep is most delicious. It is like death, a clean bath, that washes off the outer dirt."

Hastening a little with the pleasure of anticipation, he saw before him two men going slowly and disputing earnestly. Being light and soft-footed on the dusty road, he heard them as he overtook them. They were speaking of himself, and disputing whether he would reveal himself to all men and then destroy the world. He remembered the two men; he had known them in the life of his mission. But he did not disclose himself, greeting them as a stranger in the dusk, and they did not know him. He said to them:

"What then of him who would be king of the Jews and was taken and put to death for it?"

They answered suspiciously:

"Why ask you of him?"

"I have known him and thought much about him," he said.

So they replied:

"He is risen."

"Yea! And where is he and how does he live?"

"We know not, for it is not revealed. Yet he is risen and in a little while will ascend unto the Father."

"Yea! And where then is his Father?"

"Know ye not? You are then of the gentiles! The Father is in heaven, above the cloud and the firmament."

"Truly? How then will he ascend?"

"As Elijah the prophet, he shall go up in a glory."

"Even into the sky?"

"Into the sky."

"Then he is not risen in the flesh?"

"He is risen in the flesh."

"And will he take flesh up into the sky?"

"The Father in heaven will take him up."

The man who had died said no more, for his say was over, and words beget words, even as gnats. But the men asked him:

"Why do you carry a cock?"

"I am a healer," he said, "and the bird hath virtue."

"You are not a believer?"

"Yea! I believe the bird is full of life and virtue."

They walked on in silence after this, and he felt they disliked his answer. So he smiled to himself, for the weirdest phenomenon in the world is a man of narrow belief. And as they came to the outskirts of the village, the man who had died stood still in the gloaming and said in his old voice:

"Know ye me not?"

And they cried in fear:

"Master!"

"Yea!" he said, laughing softly. And he turned suddenly away down a side lane, and was gone under the wall before they knew.

So he came to an inn where the asses stood in the yard. And he called for fritters and they were made for him. So he slept under a shed. But in the morning he was wakened by a loud crowing and his cock's voice ringing in his ears. So he saw the rooster of the inn walking forth to battle, with his hens, a goodly number behind him. Then the cock of the man who had died sprang forth, and a battle began between the birds. The man of the inn ran to save his rooster, but the man who had died said:

"If my bird wins, I will give him thee. And if he lose, thou shalt eat him."

So the birds fought savagely, and the cock of the man who had died killed the common cock of the yard. Then the man who had died said to his young cock:

"Thou at least hast found thy kingdom and the females to thy body."

And he left his bird there and went on deeper into the phenomenal world, which is a vast complexity of wonders. And he asked himself a last question: "From what, and to what, could this infinite whirl be saved?"

COMMENTARY
by
Gerald M. Lacy

TABLE OF CONTENTS

I. INTRODUCTION: LAWRENCE AND THE RESURRECTION THEME

Discussions of *The Escaped Cock* frequently cite the strong parallels between the presentation of the newly risen and completed man of this novel and the life and work of Lawrence. It should come as no surprise, therefore, to find that the real beginning of Lawrence's work on the theme of what was to be his last major novel had its roots years before, that is, arose directly out of the author's near fatal illness in Mexico in early February 1925. The theme of *The Escaped Cock* was evident in Lawrence's work *at least* from 1925 to 1930, and during this final period, the symbolism and myth of resurrection appeared again and again. Not that it was a new theme; indeed, when one considers what fundamental religious and metaphysical issues are handled in the novel, and then looks back over *all* of Lawrence's fiction, poetry, and essays, this last novel appears as the completely logical culmination of Lawrence's literary career. As George Ford has pointed out,

> If this story is a kind of archetypal example of Lawrence's fiction, and if we have here a retelling of one of the oldest accounts of man's connections with God and nature, it is evident that in all of Lawrence's characteristic fiction, not merely in a story set in Biblical times, we are being exposed to a religious sense that colors the whole narrative. (*Double Measure*, p. 110)*

Indeed, *The Escaped Cock* is an "archetypal example of Lawrence's fiction," and in its "religious sense" it *is* "characteristic" of much of Lawrence's work. But what is equally significant is that this novel, coming almost at the very end of Lawrence's life, is also unique for Lawrence, both in its narrative form and in its explicit theme.

What appears to have happened is that Lawrence, near death from tuberculosis and malaria in 1925, found that he had not made explicit what was only implicit in his early works. We will probably never know the exact connection between his illness in Mexico and his writing of the unfinished "The Flying Fish." But it is significant that this story of Gethin Day, apparently driving toward a symbolic "resurrection," toward a risen man, *is* unfinished, and when we take this backward look from *The Escaped Cock*, we see that much of Lawrence's major fiction similarly appears to conclude with an "unfinished" or unresolved ending, as if the narrative energy was driving toward some unexpressed and vague resolution, a resolution felt intuitively but not expressed. One is frequently left, for example, with the feeling that the narrative is to have its "real" completion in future time with the strong implication of further important events. (And it is part of the supreme achievement of *The Escaped Cock* that even with its comparatively indeterminate ending—"Tomorrow is another day"—most critics feel that it has a kind of completeness, a finality about it, as if this parable-like story has "finished.") For example, at the end of *Sons and Lovers* (1913), Paul Morel walks alone toward the "city's gold phosphorescence" curiously unfulfilled, incomplete, but finally released for an undefined search. Ursula similarly is in a stance of waiting at the end of *The Rainbow* (1915), and even though united with Birkin in *Women in Love* (1920), she and

---

*For full references see section X, Bibliography.

123

particularly her husband still find something missing in their marriage; their happiness in union is not complete. And Lou Carrington must also wait on an isolated ranch in the mountains of New Mexico at the end of *St. Mawr* (1925) for the "mystic new man" who will "never come."

> She understood now the meaning of the Vestal Virgins, the Virgins of the holy fire in the old temples. They were symbolic of herself, of woman weary of the embrace of incompetent men, weary, weary, weary of all that, turning to the unseen gods, the unseen spirits, the hidden fire, and devoting herself to that, and that alone. Receiving thence her pacification and her fulfilment. (p. 139)

Lou tells herself:

> "Love can't really come into me from the outside, and I can never, never mate with any man, since the mystic new man will never come to me . . . . I am one of the eternal Virgins, serving the eternal fire. . . . 1 ought to stay virgin, and still, very, very still, and serve the most perfect service. I want my temple and my loneliness and my Apollo mystery of the inner fire." (pp. 139-140)

Lou is to remain inviolate until she becomes the waiting virgin priestess of Isis in *The Escaped Cock.*

Lawrence finally creates a completely "mystic new man" in the person of "the man who had died," and the curtain can only come down, the narrative tension be relaxed, and the denouement of a total literary career occur as Lawrence confronts and adapts the symbolic potential found in the Gospel account of the resurrection of Christ. Lawrence as a deeply religious man and writer is in an ancient tradition here, for most "religious" writers—particularly the moderns from Blake on—have found it necessary to work out their religious impulses in relation to the symbol or the story of Christ, to define their "religion" against not only the Christian version of resurrection, but with most of the world's known accounts of the sacred mysteries of spiritual and physical rebirth.

In the sexual and the symbolic union of the Jesus of Christianity with the virgin priestess of the Isis of Egyptian religion, Lawrence was working from his Congregationalist background and moving through the various strata of resurrection myths. He wished, it seems, to take the Western world's account of the Christian resurrection and fuse it with one of the oldest accounts of the same myth—the story of Isis and Osiris. A brief examination of this myth will indicate why it was so appealing to him.

Osiris was the offspring of the earth-god Seb and the sky-goddess Nut (the Greek names for the parents were Cronus and Rhea). He had several brothers and sisters, among them Set (who was later to betray him) and Isis (whom he later married). Osiris was a god of special importance to the Egyptians, for it was believed that he taught his people the cultivation of grains and that he was directly connected with the yearly rising and falling of the Nile, an event on which the Egyptians depended for their very lives. Set became jealous of his brother and arranged to have a special coffin built exactly to the measurements of Osiris' body. At a banquet, as a sort of a game, each male in attendance attempted to fit into the coffin, but only Osiris could fit easily. When he stretched out in the coffin, Set and his followers slammed the lid shut and flung the sealed coffin into the Nile. Isis immediately went on a search for her dead husband and finally found the coffin, miraculously grown into the trunk of a tall tree which had been cut and used as a pillar for the palace of one of the kings on the coast of Syria. Through various strategems, Isis arranged to retrieve the coffin from the pillar and returned to Egypt with the body. Set then discovered the body and cut it into fourteen pieces and scattered them throughout Egypt. Again Isis ("Isis in Search," as Lawrence pointedly calls her) dutifully sought to gather all the pieces together and to reassemble her husband's body. She found all the parts except the genitals, which had been eaten by the fish of the Nile. Isis therefore had to make an image of the phallus. Ra, the sun-god, took pity on mourning Isis and arranged to have the reassembled Osiris arise from the dead. Henceforth Osiris reigned as Lord of the Underworld, Lord of Eternity, and Ruler of the Dead. It is thus easy to understand why Osiris became a promise of resurrection and everlasting life for the Egyptians. He also function- ed as a corn-god (bringing yearly the return of flood waters and the prosperity of the crops), a tree-spirit, a god of fertility (both of nature and of man), and as a general god of the dead. (For details, see James Frazer's *The Golden Bough*, and the volume on *Adonis, Attis, and Osiris*.)

Several features of this myth would be especially appealing to Lawrence for his story of the risen man: Osiris, the dead king treacherously slain by his brother and then miraculously risen from the dead and returned to power; even though resurrected, still incomplete due to the missing phallus; the faithful and untiring search for his dismembered body by his wife Isis; Osiris in his role as the sun-god and the god of fertility of nature and of man; and finally, Osiris and Isis as the parents of Horus, the new ruler who restores harmony and well being to the kingdom of Egypt. (In regard to the latter, note Lawrence's personal emphasis in the novel: he refers to the young priestess as "Isis in Search," specif- ically not Isis as the "Mother of Horus." Lawrence can place her in her latter role in the novel *only* after the discovery of the man who had died (Osiris); here Lawrence takes a minor liberty with the Egyptian myth, for Isis was tradition- ally said to have been impregnated in a supernatural fashion by the dead Osiris *before* she discovered and reassembled his torn body.)

In the process of adapting and fusing the two accounts, Lawrence expressed the undogmatic freedom of his religious impulses and gave us an account which is as much basic and universal as it is unique. Note for example the following statements from the unpublished first draft of Part II.

"This is Isis lore, which Isis women forever will understand and only they. Aphrodite knows it not: for her the Atys, the Adonis of the afterwards is that which she has lost. And the Marys do not know it, none of the four Marys. For they never found the lost male clue to their risen man, their risen God. But Isis knew, long ago, and Isis women know today." (MS. F, pp. 9-10; for identification of MSS see below, section VII)

And several pages later:

"And many are the goddesses," she said, "but Isis alone particularly seeks her dismembered lord. And if Isis could not find the dead male, he were lost for ever, for neither Ceres nor Aphrodite nor Persephone nor even the Mary who washed your feet with tears could bring him back." (MS. F, p. 24)

Although these references to other goddesses whose roles were similar to that of Isis were omitted by Lawrence in the final version, it should be evident that he was originally remembering such parallels from his reading of Frazer's *The Golden Bough* and wishing his readers to recall them, as they *also* were to note the distinctiveness of Lawrence's portrait of Isis and the individual emphasis of his own religious vision. This new myth, bringing together in Part II Christian and non-Christian elements, is obviously post-Christian; it is also more a philosophical movement beyond Christianity than it is a direct frontal assault on the present Christian church. It proposes a correction and reform much more than it criticizes.

Lawrence—like Blake—saw an incongruity between two opposing interpretations of the central belief of Christianity and felt an urgent need for a basic reform. He believed that "church doctrine teaches the resurrection of the body; and if that doesn't mean the whole man, what does it mean?" (Letter of 7 January 1929; Huxley, p. 778. See also "The Risen Lord" in *Phoenix II*) Compare this statement to the logical and rational attempts of Augustine to reconcile "the evil of lust—a word which, though applicable to many vices, is especially appropriate to sexual uncleanness," and "the shame which attends all sexual intercourse" (*The City of God*, Bk. XIV, ch. 16 and 18) with what he believes is a divinely created physical body. This fundamental disagreement is essentially the difference in emphasis between the spirit of Christ and the Gospels and the rigid and rational precepts of Paul and Augustine. Like Gide, Lawrence saw this as a dangerous underlying conflict; *The Escaped Cock* is his answer. When one recalls its enormous influence, Augustine's *City of God*, along with the more usually cited volume of Frazer's *Adonis, Attis, and Osiris*, is illuminating reading in relation to this novel, for to borrow a phrase from Maurice Friedman's *To Deny Our Nothingness*, it is what Lawrence saw as the "inauthenticity" of the Augustinian tradition in the Christian church which pointed to an "authentic model for modern man."

Lawrence tells us in the late autobiographical essay "Hymns in a Man's Life" (August 1928) that "by the time I was sixteen I had criticized and got over the Christian dogma" (*Phoenix II*, p. 599) and in a letter of 27 October 1925 to John Middleton Murry, Lawrence's estranged friend who was then working on his *Life of Christ*, Lawrence wrote ". . . must you really write about Jesus? Jesus becomes more unsympathisch to me the longer I live: crosses and nails and tears and all that stuff! I think he shoved us into a nice cul-de-sac." (Murry, *Reminiscences*, p. 193) From his early rejection of the inauthentic and life-denying dogma—if not the "wonder" and emotion of Christianity, which he lyrically praises in "Hymns in a Man's Life,"—and his weariness with the stifling, over-dramatic presentation of Christ, Lawrence attempted in *The Escaped Cock* to get out of that "nice cul-de-sac." It would be true to say, I think, that the figure of Jesus had long been a serious impediment to Lawrence's religious vision, and the surmounting of this obstacle would consume much of his creative energy during the last years of his life. This effort began explicitly with the moving language of Lawrence's unfinished story "The Flying Fish," the first part of which was dictated by the sick author to his wife in the spring of 1925, just a few months before his October letter to Murry, and with the symbolic restoration found in "Sun," written shortly after Lawrence returned to the

Mediterranean he loved. Both "The Flying Fish" (March-April 1925) and "Sun" (November-December 1925) are obviously related thematically to *The Escaped Cock* and these two stories serve as a kind of prelude to the full expressive movement of the novel. The next section of the commentary will deal directly with this relationship.

As has been suggested above, one of Lawrence's central concerns had been to portray in his work a new vision, for he believed that man could not live "with a vision that is not true to his inner experience and inner feeling." This is from "The Risen Lord" (July, 1929), an essay which Keith Sagar has called "a third part" of *The Escaped Cock*, and which serves as a summing up of Lawrence's life-long religious struggle. In it, Lawrence argues passionately for his belief in "the only part of the great mystery" which the church has failed to teach.

> The Churches loudly assert: We preach Christ crucified!—But in so doing, they preach only half of the Passion, and do only half their duty. The Creed says: "Was crucified, dead, and buried . . . the third day He rose again from the dead." And again, "I believe in the resurrection of the body . . ." So that to preach Christ Crucified is to preach half the truth. It is the business of the Church to preach Christ born among men—which is Christmas; Christ Crucified, which is Good Friday; and Christ Risen, which is Easter. And after Easter, till November and All Saints, and till Annunciation, the year belongs to the Risen Lord: that is, all the full-flowering spring, all summer, and the autumn of wheat and fruit, all belong to Christ Risen.
>
> But the Churches insist on Christ Crucified, and rob us of the blossom and fruit of the year. The Catholic Church, which has given us our images, has given us the Christ-child, in the lap of woman, and again, Christ Crucified: then the Mass, the mystery of atonement through sacrifice. Yet all this is really preparatory, these are the preparatory stages of the real living religion. The Christ-child, enthroned in the lap of the Mother, is obviously only a preparatory image, to prepare us for Christ the Man. Yet a vast mass of Christians stick there. (*Phoenix II*, p. 571)

Lawrence follows this with a separation of mankind into "three great image-divisions."

> We have the old and the elderly, who never were exposed to the guns, still fatuously maintaining that man is the Christ-child and woman the infallible safeguard from all evil and all danger. It is fatuous, because it absolutely didn't work. Then we have the men of middle age, who were all tortured and virtually put to death by the war. They accept Christ Crucified as their image, are essentially womanless, and take the great cry: *Consummatum est!—It is finished!*—as their last word.— Thirdly, we have the young, who never went through the war. They have no illusions about it, however, and the death-cry of their elder generation: *It is finished!* rings cold through their blood. They cannot answer. They cannot even scoff. It is no joke, and never will be a joke. (Ibid., pp. 572-573)

Lawrence can accept most of the central mysteries of the church, but he wants us to accept, with all its implications, "Christ risen in the full flesh!"

> We must accept the image complete, if we accept it at all. We must take the mystery in its fulness and in fact. It is only the image of our own experience. Christ rises, when He rises from the dead, in the flesh, not merely as spirit. He rises with hands and feet, as Thomas knew for certain: and if with hands and feet, then with lips and stomach and genitals of a man. Christ risen, and risen in the whole of His flesh, not with some left out.
>
> Christ risen in the full flesh! What for? It is here the gospels are all vague and faltering, and the Churches leave us in the lurch. . . .
>
> It is the only part of the great mystery which is all wrong. The virgin birth, the baptism, the temptation, the teaching, Gethsemane, the betrayal, the crucifixion, the burial and the resurrection, these are all true according to our inward experience. They are what men and women go through, in their different ways. But floated up into heaven as flesh-and-blood, and never set down again—this nothing in all our experience will ever confirm. (Ibid., p. 574)

And finally:

> If Jesus rose from the dead in triumph, a man on earth triumphant in renewed flesh, triumphant over the mechanical anti-life convention of Jewish priests, Roman despotism, and universal money-lust; triumphant above all over His own self-absorption, self-consciousness, self-importance; triumphant and free as a man in full flesh and full, final experience, even the accomplished acceptance of His own death; a man at last full and free in flesh and soul, a man at one with death: then He rose to become at one with life, to live the great life of the flesh and the soul together, as peonies or foxes do, in their lesser way. If Jesus rose as a full man, in full flesh and soul, then He rose to take a woman to Himself, to live with her, and to know the tenderness and blossoming of the twoness with her; He who had been hitherto so limited to His oneness, or His universality, which is the same thing. If Jesus rose in the full flesh, He rose to know the tenderness of a woman, and the great pleasure of her, and to have children by her. (Ibid., p. 575)

This is the philosphy (or "metaphysic," to use Lawrence's word) which reached its ultimate expression in *The Escaped Cock*. In the following section I shall trace the chronological sequence of events which lead to the composition of this novel, beginning with February 1925 and with relationships which are most evident with the second "phallic" part of what was to become *The Escaped Cock*. Thus Part II will be discussed before Part I.

II. CHRONOLOGY: INFLUENCES AND WORKS

Lawrence planned to return to Europe from Oaxaca, Mexico, in February 1925, but shortly after completing *The Plumed Serpent*, he fell very ill with influenza and malaria. A man near death, he struggled with his wife to Mexico City and received some much-needed medical attention, and on the advice of his doctors, the Lawrences decided to return to the more healthy atmosphere of their Taos, New Mexico, ranch. Sometime during his slow recovery, probably while he was still in Mexico, Lawrence began work on "The Flying Fish." After the return to Taos, he corrected the proofs for *St. Mawr*, completed revisions in the manuscript of *The Plumed Serpent* and wrote *David*, his last complete play. But it is the unfinished "The Flying Fish" which concerns us most. This is a story of a man, Gethin Day, ill in body and spirit (both are "as good as dead with the malaria") who leaves Mexico to return to Europe. He has with him a copy of a mystical and symbolic sixteenth century manuscript, a *Book of Days*, which he reads as he slowly recovers from his soul-weariness and illness.

"For the little day is like a house with the family round the hearth, and the door shut. Yet outside whispers the Greater Day, wall-less, and heartless. And the time will come at last when the walls of the little day shall fall, and what is left of the family of men shall find themselves outdoors in the Greater Day, houseless and abroad, even here between the knees of the Vales, even in Crichdale. It is a doom that will come upon tall men. And then they will breathe deep, and be breathless in the great air, and salt sweat will stand on their brow, thick as buds on sloe-bushes when the sun comes back. And little men will shudder and die out, like clouds of grasshoppers falling in the sea. Then tall men will remain alone in the land, moving deeper in the Greater Day, and moving deeper. Even as the flying fish, when he leaves the air and recovereth his element in the depth, plunges and invisibly rejoices. So will tall men rejoice, after their flight of fear, through the thin air, pursued by death. For it is on wings of fear, sped from the mouth of death, that the flying fish riseth twinkling in the air, and rustles in astonishment silvery through the thin small day. But he dives again into the great peace of the deeper day, and under the belly of death, and passes into his own." (*Phoenix*, pp. 785-6)

Much of the "greater day" imagery here, as well as its implicit statement of a theme of resurrection and rebirth, appears again in *The Escaped Cock*. This fact is central to a study of the novel, for it suggests that the final formative phase of the salient theme of Lawrence's career took place shortly after his near death and carried over to the novel. Later Gethin reappraises his own condition.

. . . he was, in the words of his ancestor, aware of the Greater Day showing through the cracks in the ordinary day. And it was useless trying to fill up the cracks. The little day was destined to crumble away, as far as he was concerned, and he would *have* to inhabit the greater day. The very sight of the volcano cone in mid-air made him know it. His little self was used up, worn out. He felt sick and frail, facing this change of life. (Ibid., p. 788)

129

This reluctance to emerge from a death-in-life is much like the feeling of the man who had died as he awakens in the tomb.

> He could move if he wanted: he knew that. But he had no want. Who would want to come back from the dead? A deep, deep nausea stirred in him, at the premonition of movement. He resented already the fact of the strange, incalculable moving that had already taken place in him: the moving back into consciousness. He had not wished it. He had wanted to stay outside, in the place where even memory is stone dead.

Gethin Day never reaches England, for the story was never completed by Lawrence—perhaps due to his illness, perhaps because he was not yet ready to complete the theme. Some years later, however, he told the Brewsters that "the last part will be regenerate man, a real life in this Garden of Eden." (Brewster, p. 288) This is obviously the theme of *The Escaped Cock*, a story of a "regenerate man," told with much emphasis on the differences between the "greater day" and the lesser day. (See, for example, pp. 44 and 50 of the present volume.)

Lawrence recovered from his illness and arrived in England on 30 September 1925. He wrote to Murry the next day, but the two men did not meet until Murry visited London on 28 October, the day before the Lawrences left for Germany. Murry describes this encounter as follows.

> . . . we met at Gower Street, and he attacked me for writing about Jesus, I stood my ground quite firmly against him, saying that for me Jesus had finally come to represent the highest achievement of humanity. It wasn't a matter for argument any more with me. What we had to do was to understand him, and go on to be different.
>
> Lawrence was rather impressed. He pressed me hard to know what I thought of Judas. And I told him that he was the only one of the disciples who understood Jesus; and that Jesus knew that he was the only one who understood. I was sure that Judas killed himself because there had been no glorious manifestation of the Messiah and the Reign of God at the Crucifixion; and that the whole story of the "betrayal" was the invention of those who did not understand the relation between the two men. It was Judas's horror at the failure, at the uselessness of the final suffering of Jesus, at which he had connived, that made him kill himself. It was not, in him, "the mystery of iniquity" at all. He was the broken-hearted lover. (Murry, p. 196)

Lawrence wrote to Murry on 31 October, two days after their meeting.

> I read your November *Adelphi*. Don't you see there still *has* to be a Creator? Jesus is not the Creator, even of himself. And we have to go on being created. By the Creator.—More important to me than Jesus. But of course God-the-Father, the Dieu Père, is a bore. Jesus is as far as one can go with God, anthropomorphically. After that no more anthropos.
>
> Perhaps I'll write you a little article. (Murry, p. 195)

Murry's comments on his own interpretation of the relationship between

Judas and Jesus should be compared with the portrayal of Judas in *The Escaped Cock*:

> "Oh Madeleine, I want to take my single way in life, which is my portion. My public life is over, the life of my conviction and my mission, the life of my self-importance. Now I can wait on life, and say nothing, and have no one betray me. I wanted to be greater than the limits of my hands and feet, so I brought betrayal on myself. And I know I wronged Judas, my poor Judas. Now I know. He died as I died, my poor Judas. For I have died, and now I know my own limits. Now I can live without striving to sway others any more. For my reach ends in my finger-tips, and my stride is no longer than the ends of my toes. Yet I would embrace multitudes, I who have never truly embraced even one woman, or one man. But Judas and the high priests delivered me from my own salvation, and I am no longer a lover of multitudes."

The *final* importance of Murry's possible influence on *The Escaped Cock* may be slight, but Lawrence's letter to and meeting with him are the first indications that Lawrence was beginning to think seriously of the potential in the Christ story and of writing about it.

During the next month, Lawrence wrote "Sun." On 25 November 1925 he wrote to his artist friend Dorothy Brett:

> Dear Brett
> You've got the real doldrums. But one always feels bad, the first few days when one comes to Italy. It's sunny here, and the sun is hot; but *very* windy. . . .
> There is something I like very much about the Mediterranean; it relaxes one, after the tension of America. Wait a bit, till you get used to it, and you'll like it too. . . . I'm enclosing two litle MSS.—one for Spud. Make one carbon copy, will you. . . . (*Collected Letters*, pp. 867-868; hereafter referred to as CL)

The two manuscripts Lawrence sent were almost certainly "A Little Moonshine With Lemon" and the first part of "Sun." The two pieces are excellent contrasts—the vital power of the hot sun's dazzling light and the cool peace of moon memories, a bitter-sweet nostalgia for the past. On 17 December 1925 he received the typescript of the first part of "Sun." The completed manuscript was sent to Curtis Brown by 6 January 1926, and on 9 January 1926, Lawrence wrote to Murry: "The *sun* means a lot. It's almost *the grace of God* in itself." (CL p. 878, italics added) The life-giving, restoring value of the phallic sun is the central image in the short story "Sun," and Lawrence suggests that this healing radiance has something like "the grace of God" when he describes the sun's effect on Juliet: ". . . the sun was gradually penetrating her to know her in the cosmic carnal sense of the word. . . ." The sun-wrought alteration in Juliet is much like the effect of the man who had died on the priestess of Isis. For example, the parallels between the short story and the novel are unmistakable when one compares "Sun" with the first draft of Part II (MS. F).

So she lay in the sun, but not for long, for it was getting strong, fierce. And in spite of herself, the bud that had been tight and deep immersed in the innermost gloom of her, was rearing, rearing and straightening its curved stem, to open its dark tips and show a gleam of rose. Her womb was coming open wide with rosy ecstasy, like a lotus flower. ("Sun," unexpurgated text, *The Princess and Other Stories*, pp. 128-129)

In the novel, the young priestess of Isis is warned by a slave of the intrusion of a possible malefactor, but she realizes with immediate clairvoyance that this is no common criminal, no common man. When she views the man who had died, the beginnings of her renewal are described with a very similar "blossoming" metaphor:

It was the peculiar pure stillness of the greater peace which seemed revealed in every outline, and which gave the poignant, piercing sense of beauty to the woman's soul, to her womb. Her womb with keen unusedness, keen to pain, began to stir, began to raise its head as a lotus-bud raises its head, towards the strange fate of flowering. (MS. F, p. 12)

With the restoration in the present text of a phrase hitherto omitted from Part II (italicized in the following quotation), the parallels in imagery are more evident than in earlier editions:

For the first time, she was touched on the quick at the sight of a man, as if the tip of a fine flame of living had touched her. It was the first time. Men had roused all kinds of feelings in her, but never had touched her *on the yearning quick of her womb*, with the flame-tip of life.

But the similarities are much more evident when we find from the manuscripts that in the first draft of Part II the sexual culmination of the man who had died and the priestess of Isis occurs in a "sun-room."

So she went with him slowly to the sun-room, which was shaped like a shell arching softly in a concave towards the south-east sun; like a shallow cave, like a scallop-shell, it faced the sun. It was built for taking sun-baths, in the morning, to make the body softly rosy.

And the winter sun shone off the sea, looking into the scallop shell. And he was pure with his own fire, and lordly, and his touch was divine. This was a day with one of the sheer pure suns of the greater day, beyond commonness of littleness. Greatness and beauty of the greater day was on the hills, and on the tree all white with bloom and glistening, and on the yellow flowers of the earth, and on the uprising thick buds of the asphodel, and on the white shore, and the strong blue sea of winter. Splendour, the uprisen splendour of the greater day, risen and pouring forth from the magnificent sun. . . .

She knew herself unfolded and radiating like the lotus, under the double sunshine of day and of man, the dark, cleaving sunshine of the man penetrating in fine rays of passion into the soft gold heart of her lotus, the darkly-opened womb, his sun-heat beating into her blossom,

132

and over them both, the lordly sunshine of the winter day. (MS. F, pp. 26-27, 32)

The sun imagery of "Sun" and the "greater day" metaphor of "The Flying Fish," both written in 1925 and both with only a tacit "resurrection" (notice the last sentence in "Sun": ". . . and there was no Perseus in the universe to cut the bonds.") are highly important to *The Escaped Cock*, as the above quotation makes evident. A proper resurrection myth is not yet possible for Lawrence, for he has to find his "Perseus," his "regenerate man." But he is moving toward that discovery—almost, it seems, against his will.

The next important event which contributes to the development of the resurrection theme occurred when Lawrence saw Brett's painting of Jesus in March 1926. He already knew about her work and this painting, having written her in January: "I am surprised at your adding one more to the list of Crucifixion. Whom are you popping on the Cross, to make him say 'too late'?" (CL, p. 882) Lawrence's interest in Brett's painting and her portrayal of Jesus appears in several subsequent letters.

How is your Primrose Jesus getting on? I hear Murry's *Life of Jesus* was to appear in one of Lord Beaverbrook's papers . . . . (CL, p. 884)

Sorry the Brewsters snubbed your Jesus. Practise the tiger and the cheetah before you do your Buddah. The beast comes first. (CL, p. 887)

On 27 February Lawrence arrived at Villa Quatro Venti, Capri, and sometime between then and 7 March he first saw his friend's painting and discovered whom she was "popping on the Cross." Brett has described the occasion vividly ("you" is Lawrence, to whom she addressed her memoir):

The Brewsters are packing for India, box after box. Earl is tired out. You have come down to the hotel to see my picture. I have perched it on the bed, in the best light available. You look at it in astonishment; then you laugh and say quickly:
"It's a good idea, but it's much too like me—much too like."
"I know," I reply, "but I took the heads half from you and half from John the Baptist."
"It's too like me," you repeat abruptly. "You will have to change it. Also put a little more pink in the sunset: it's too golden. Just a touch of pink would help. But wherever did you get the idea from?"
"I don't know—it just came. It seemed to come from you, to be you."
The picture is of a crucifixion. The pale yellow Christ hangs on the Cross, against an orange sunset. With that final spurt of strength before death, he is staring at the vision of the figure in front of him. His eyes are visionary, his figure tense and aware. Before him, straddled across a rock, half-curious, half-smiling, is the figure of Pan, holding up a bunch of grapes to the dying Christ: a dark, reddish-gold figure with horns and hoofs. The heads of Pan and Christ are both your head. (Brett, p. 275)

All of these events—the work on "The Flying Fish" and "Sun," the meeting and conversation with Murry, and the discovery of Brett's painting—made it likely, if not inevitable, that Lawrence would become more and more aware of the necessity of completing his own concept of a resurrection myth by re-considering the life of Christ and then adapting it to his own philosophy. For example, in a letter of 8 March 1927, over a year after seeing Brett's painting, Lawrence told her that he too had started to paint "a resurrection," but by 24 March he wrote her "I shan't do a crucifixion, even with Pan to put his fingers to his nose at the primrose Jesus. Damn crosses!" (CL, pp. 968, 970) Lawrence was not able, not willing apparently, to resume work on his "resurrection" painting until late in May, just *after* his completion of Part I of "The Escaped Cock," and unlike Brett, he would never paint a "crucifixion." When we consider the difference between the two great religious symbols—the cruci-fixion and the resurrection—and compare them to the events noted above, a pattern of two parallel themes, two dominant themes which can only *merge* in *The Escaped Cock*, becomes apparent. We should recall from the first sec-tion of the Commentary that Lawrence had always had a deep religious sense in his works, particularly one which had a "searching" quality, an implicit theme of resurrection. "The Flying Fish" and "Sun" fit this thematic line. But he had early abandoned the dogma and particularly the crucifixion of Christianity—"the Crucifixion of Christ is a great mucking about with part of the symbolism of a great religious Vision." (CL, p. 302) This last remark was written in 1914, shortly after Lawrence had completed the autobiographical novel *Sons and Lovers*. In this novel, Paul Morel (Lawrence) "was setting now full sail towards Agnosticism, but such a religious Agnosticism. . . ." (p. 227) He was undergoing an important transition:

> Religion was fading into the background. He had shovelled away all the beliefs that would hamper him, had cleared the ground, and come more or less to the bedrock of belief that one should feel inside one-self for right and wrong, and should have the patience to gradually realise one's God. (p. 256)

And the great "sin" in the novel and a main part of the painful story of Paul Morel's growth into manhood is that his first love Miriam (Lawrence's first love, Jessie Chambers) had wanted to sacrifice herself to "a Christ in him." Lawrence's life-long quarrel with Christianity had thus centered primarily on the pre-eminence of the Crucifixion and the formidable figure of Christ. This is the second thematic line, and its merging and resolution with the first thematic line was very likely provoked or induced by the meeting and conver-sation with Murry and Brett's startling painting. Lawrence wrote in 1914 that

> . . . the moderns today prefer to end insisting on the sad plight. It is characteristic of us that we have preserved, of a trilogy which was really Prometheus Unbound, only the Prometheus Bound and terribly suffering on the rock of his own egotism.
> But the great souls in all time did not end there. In the mediaeval period, Christianity did *not* insist on the Cross: but on the Resurrec-tion: churches were built to the glorious hope of resurrection. Now we think we are very great, whilst we enumerate the smarts of the crucifixion. We are too mean to get any further.
> I think there is the dual way of looking at things: our way, which is to say '*I* am all. All other things are but radiation out from me.'— The other way is to try to conceive the whole, to build up a whole by

134

means of symbolism, because symbolism avoids the I and puts aside the egotist; and, in the whole, to take our decent place. That was how man built the cathedrals. He didn't say 'out of my breast springs this cathedral!' But 'in this vast whole I am a small part, I move and live and have my being.'

. . . .

But Christianity should teach us now, that after our Crucifixion, and the darkness of the tomb, we shall rise again in the flesh, you, I, as we are today, resurrected in the bodies, and acknowledging the Father, and glorying in his power, like Job.

It is very dangerous to use these old terms lest they sound like cant. But if only one can grasp and know again as a new truth, true for ones own history, the great vision, the great, satisfying conceptions of the world's greatest periods, it is enough. Because so it is made new.

All religions I think have the same inner conception, with different expressions. (CL, pp. 301-303)

The influence of Murry and Brett alone would likely have not stimulated Lawrence to a merging of the two thematic lines. The old terms in themselves were dangerously close to "cant"; the suitable "symbolism" was lacking; and Lawrence had not found an expression of the eternal truth made "true for ones own history." He found, however, all of these things in the Etruscan tombs, the next important influence on the final narrative expression of Lawrence's religious vision, *The Escaped Cock*.

Lawrence had expressed an interest in writing a book on the Etruscans as early as April 1926. A walking tour of the Etruscan sites, made convenient and easily accessible by a move to the Villa Mirenda near Florence in May, was planned but had to be postponed because of Lawrence's return to England in the summer of 1926. But the spring of 1927 found Lawrence back in the Villa Mirenda, where he and his friend Earl Brewster now made fresh plans.

On 5 April, Lawrence and Brewster were in Rome, looking at the magnificent collection of Etruscan artifacts at the Villa Giulia. Most of this collection represents Etruscan funerary art, but Lawrence was deeply impressed by the brilliant sense of life, not death, which he found throughout his Etruscan trip. It was "neither an ecstasy of bliss, a heaven, nor a purgatory of torment. It was just a natural continuance of the fullness of life. Everything was in terms of life, of living." (*Etruscan Places*, p. 109) Lawrence grew up in a religious tradition which stressed the crucifixion, not the resurrection. Amidst the ruins and tombs of a dead civilization, an ancient civilization destroyed by the "expansion with a big E" of modern-like Roman empire, Lawrence found a "delicate sensitiveness," "a wonderful touch of vital life, of life significance," and a "real Etruscan liveliness and naturalness." It was life, and the continuance of life beyond death which impressed Lawrence. Here was a culture for whose religious feeling he could feel a great affinity; here was a cultural emphasis upon resurrection. The depictions of Etruscan life and religion which he saw at Cerveteri, Tarquinia, Vulci, and Volterra represented a refreshing escape from the "cul-de-sac" of Christianity.

On Easter Sunday, 1927, Lawrence and Earl Brewster, pausing in their tour of the ancient Etruscan cities north of Rome, passed a shop window in Volterra. Brewster recalled this day:

My memory is that Easter Morning found us at Grosseto: there we passed a little shop, in the window of which was a toy white rooster escaping from an egg. I remarked that it suggested a title—"The Escaped Cock—a story of the Resurrection." Lawrence replied that he had been thinking about writing a story of the Resurrection: later in the book of that title which he gave me, he has written: "To Earl this story, that began in Volterra, when we were there together." I am inclined to think *The Escaped Cock* the most beautiful writing Lawrence has left us, but I doubt the adequacy of its title, for which I myself might be blamed. (Brewster, pp. 123-124)

But with this recollection we can now compare Lawrence's previously unpublished statement to Harry and Caresse Crosby, written in Lawrence's hand on a sheet between Part I and Part II when he presented them with the holograph manuscript of the novel.

"MS. of the story afterward called The Escaped Cock—Part I—written in the Villa Mirenda near Florence in 1927, Easter, & suggested by a little Easter toy of a cock escaping from a man, seen in a shop window—in Volterra the week before Easter—after looking at Etruscan tombs.
Now given to Harry Crosby, because we decided the fate of the story in the upper room of the Mill, on Easter Sunday 1929.
DHL
I typed this story out myself, so probably I altered it in typescript a good bit. (MSS. A & G, bound manuscript)

This statement was almost certainly written on 20 May 1929 as Lawrence's letter of that date to Harry Crosby indicates. Brewster's account, on the other hand, was published years later in 1934. The two explanations differ in most of their essentials, and at least two of Brewster's three assertions are incorrect. Easter fell on 17 April in 1927; Lawrence returned to Florence from his Etruscan trip on Monday, 11 April. Lawrence could have been in Grosseto on Palm Sunday, 10 April, but he was almost certainly in Volterra on that day, as *Etruscan Places* indicates; a letter (3 May 1927) to Brewster also places the shop window in Volterra. As Brewster's description appears to be wrong in regard to the place and the date, and as Lawrence is accurate and consistent in his statements, whom are we to believe about the exact nature of the toy? The toy-as-egg is more easily imagined as an Easter toy, but the toy-as-rooster-escaping-from-man exactly fits the story pattern as we now have it. Thus it is tempting to dismiss Brewster's account as unreliable in this respect as in the others, although all that can be claimed with absolute certainty is that there is a fundamental confusion about one of the formative images which lies behind the inception of *The Escaped Cock*.

The day after he returned from his Etruscan trip, Lawrence mentioned in a letter of 12 April that "I always labor at the same thing, to make the sex relation valid and precious, instead of shameful." This is an explicit reference to *Lady Chatterley's Lover*, but it could easily be applied to one of the themes of *The Escaped Cock*, a theme which must have already begun to form in Lawrence's imagination. On the next day, 13 April 1927, he received a copy of V. V. Rozanov's *Solitaria* from his friend S. S. Koteliansky. *Solitaria* was, according to Lawrence's review (see *Phoenix*, pp. 367-371), "a sort of philosophical work, about a hundred pages, of a kind not uncommon in Russia, consisting in fragmentary jottings of thoughts which occurred to the author, mostly during the years 1910 and 1911 . . . ." But what is most important for our interests: "The book is an attack on Christianity. . . . Rozanov has more or less recovered the genuine pagan vision, the phallic vision, and with those eyes he looks, in amazement and consternation, on the mess of Christianity." There is also a reference to Jesus in a contemporaneous letter of 14 April 1927 to Mabel Dodge Luhan. (Lawrence refers to this date as Good Friday, but Good Friday, 1927 was 15 April.)

> As for a change of life—there's a very nice poem on it somewhere at the ranch—if somebody hasn't torn it out from the end of one of my books of MS. When it comes to changes, there's nothing to be done but to accept 'em and go through with them and put up with the penalty of them, in the hopes of coming through into calmer water. Myself, I'm in just the same way—just simply suffering from a change of life, and a queer sort of recoil, as if one's whole soul were drawing back from connection with everything. This is the day they put Jesus in the tomb—and really, those three days in the tomb begin to have a terrible significance and reality to me. And the resurrection is an unsatisfactory business—just *noli me tangere* and no more. Poveri noi! But pazienza! The wheel will go round. . . . I feel for the time a sort of soreness, physical, mental, and spiritual, which is no doubt change of life, and I wish it would pass off. I think it is passing off. Meanwhile pazienza! But till it heals up, I don't feel like making much effort in any direction. It is *easiest* here. (Luhan, p. 326)

This letter clearly exhibits the closeness between this period of Lawrence's life and his story of the risen man. The other and perhaps more pertinent disclosures in this letter are the references to Jesus and the Resurrection and the disclosure that Lawrence now feels that "those three days in the tomb *begin* to have a terrible *significance* and *reality* to me" (italics added). It is evident that he is now thinking a great deal about the figure of Christ, together with his persistent interest in a viable resurrection myth, and with this letter it is very likely that we are at the beginning of *The Escaped Cock*. By 25 April Lawrence was working on his "resurrection story." The story was completed—at least the first draft—by 3 May. Thus he wrote the entire story (the *Forum* draft, Part I) in from one to three weeks. He had left off working on his resurrection painting the last week in March; he began work on it again on 27 May.

Lawrence's Rozanov review and its possible influence on *The Escaped Cock* and *Lady Chatterley's Lover* have been discussed at length in an article by George Zytaruk, "The Phallic Vision: D. H. Lawrence and V. V. Rozanov" (*Comparative Literature Studies*, 4 [1967]: 283-97). Two days after Lawrence's first mention of his work on his "resurrection story," he completed the Rozanov review and returned it to Koteliansky.

When Zytaruk wrote his article, he did not have access to the complete Koteliansky letters (which he has since edited), and he could not be clear as to when Lawrence actually wrote the review of *Solitaria*. From the letters now available, we can tell that the review was finished within two weeks after Lawrence received his copy of *Solitaria*, and coincided with the writing of the early version of "The Escaped Cock." Zytaruk suggests that Lawrence, for the first time, speaks unequivocally in the Rozanov review of the "phallic vision." This may be true, but this view stresses the importance of Rozanov and tends to slight the enthusiastic response of Lawrence to his Etruscan trip with Brewster. What *is* significant about *Solitaria* is that its "phallic vision" is yoked to a criticism of Christianity, and as Zytaruk later says, the Rozanov review confirmed Lawrence's artistic intuition that he was headed in the right direction. Zytaruk refers to the passage from *Solitaria* in which Rozanov, in effect, throws a "challenge," in the form of the enormous effort required to overcome the centuries-old image of Christ, and he suggests that Lawrence took up the challenge in *The Escaped Cock*. This is highly probable. But certainly the Etruscan trip was even more challenging, and this is evident when we consider a theme which runs throughout *Etruscan Places*.

Lawrence did not begin writing the first Etruscan essay until early June, a few months after the composition of "The Escaped Cock," but when we read *Etruscan Places* and recall that the short story was written immediately after Lawrence's return from the actual Etruscan trip, we are aware of an analogous temper of mind and import in the two books.

It was the extraordinary contrast between other civilizations and the Etruscan which first deeply impressed Lawrence when he arrived at Cerveteri.

> There is a queer stillness and a curious peaceful repose about the Etruscan places I have been to, quite different from the weirdness of Celtic places, the slightly repellent feeling of Rome and the old Campagna, and the rather horrible feeling of the great pyramid places in Mexico, Teotihuacan and Cholula, and Mitla in the south; or the amiably idolatrous Buddha places in Ceylon. There is a stillness and a softness in these great grassy mounds with their ancient stone girdles, and down the central walk there lingers still a kind of homeliness and happiness. True, it was a still and sunny afternoon in April, and larks rose from the soft grass of the tombs. But there was a stillness and a soothingness in all the air, in that sunken place, and a feeling that it was good for one's soul to be there. (*Etruscan Places*, pp. 105-106)

And in contrast to what might be expected in a necropolis—

> The tombs seem so easy and friendly, cut out of rock underground. One does not feel oppressed, descending into them. It must be partly owing to the peculiar charm of natural proportion which is in all Etruscan things of the unspoilt, unromanized centuries. There is a simplicity, combined with a most peculiar, free-breasted naturalness and spontaneity, in the shapes and movements of the underworld walls and spaces, that at once reassures the spirit. The Greeks sought to make an impression, and Gothic still more seeks to impress the mind. The Etruscans, no. The things they did, in their easy centuries, are as natural and as easy as breathing. They leave the breast breathing freely and pleasantly, with a certain fullness of life. Even the tombs. And that is the true Etruscan quality: ease, naturalness, and an abundance of life, no need to force the mind or the soul in any direction. (Ibid., pp. 108-109)

Lawrence goes to great length to explain his own reaction to the numerous Etruscan symbols—"the phallic stone," the "carved stone house" which symbolized "the womb, the *arx*, where life retreats in the last refuge. . . . in which lies the mystery of eternal life, the manna and the mysteries," and finally the heraldic animals found in the tomb painting—dolphins, ducks, fish, birds, lions and deer. It is in this latter respect that Lawrence found the Etruscan religion to differ from Christianity:

> The Etruscan religion, surely, was never anthropomorphic: that is, whatever gods it contained were not *beings*, but symbols of elemental powers, just symbols: as was the case earlier in Egypt. The undivided Godhead, if we can call it such, was symbolized by the *mundum*, the plasm-cell with its nucleus: that which is the very beginning; instead of, as with us, by a personal god, a person being the very end of all creation or evolution. So it is all the way through: the Etruscan religion is concerned with all those physical and creative powers and forces which go to the building up and the destroying of the soul: the soul, the personality, being that which gradually is produced out of chaos, like a flower, only to disappear again into chaos, or the underworld. We, on the contrary, say: In the beginning was the Word!—and deny the physical universe true existence, We exist only in the Word, which is beaten out thin to cover, gild, and hide all things. (Ibid., p. 165)

If the Rozanov review had impressed him with its cogent attack on the "mess of Christianity," what Lawrence saw of the ruins of the Etruscan civilization— particularly "the Etruscan liveliness [which] was a religion of life . . . a conception of the universe and man's place in the universe which made men live to the depth of their capacity," and the "Etruscan vitality, beautiful with the mystery of the unrifled ark, ripe with the phallic knowledge and the Etruscan carelessness"—offered him an opportunity to view a culture and a religion, perhaps the only one, whose whole "pulse and rhythm" was compatible with his own. It was like a refreshing breath after the stagnancy of a materialistic modern society severely lacking in any "religion of life."

The Etruscan religion of life, on the other hand, stressed living and resurrection after death, the continuance of life, the ever on-flowing stream of the life force. This was something much more than a hell, purgatory, or heaven. It was something truly infinite, truly eternal. Lawrence discovered a symbolic representation of this in two symbols which he found in the painted tombs of Tarquinia. The first was the "mysterious egg" which "the man who had died" (note the connection in this phrase with *The Escaped Cock*) holds in a banquet scene depicted on the wall of the Tomb of the Lioness:

> He holds up the egg of resurrection, within which the germ sleeps as the soul sleeps in the tomb, before it breaks the shell and emerges again. (Ibid., p. 142)

(Perhaps we should recall here Brewster's recollection of the "toy" of a cock escaping from an egg.) The second symbol was the sacred round saucer, the *patera* or *mundum*

which represents the round germ of heaven and earth. It stands for the plasm, also, of the living cell, with its nucleus, which is the indivisible God of the beginning, and which remains alive and unbroken to the end, the eternal quick of all things, which yet divides and sub-divides, so that it becomes the sun of the firmament and the lotus of the waters under the earth, and the rose of all existence upon the earth: and the sun maintains its own quick, unbroken for ever; and there is a living quick of the sea, and of all waters; and every living created thing has its own unfailing quick. So within each man is the quick of him, when he is a baby, and when he is old, the same quick; some spark, some unborn and undying vivid life-electron. And this is what is symbolized in the *patera*, which may be made to flower like a rose or like the sun, but which remains the same, the germ central with the living plasm. (Ibid., p. 127)

Much of this symbolism of life continually opening and unfolding to life is also found in *The Escaped Cock*.

Men after the Etruscans, however, had lost the "touch" of the Etruscans, their closeness to an undying natural life force. Again we are aware of Lawrence's criticism of man's deteriorating religious sense.

The old religion of the profound attempt of man to harmonize himself with nature, and hold his own and come to flower in the great seething of life, changed with the Greeks and Romans into a desire to resist nature, to produce a mental cunning and a mechanical force that would outwit Nature and chain her down completely, completely, till at last there should be nothing free in nature at all, all should be controlled, domesticated, put to man's meaner uses. Curiously enough, with the idea of the triumph over nature arose the idea of a gloomy Hades, a hell and purgatory. To the people of the great natural religions the after-life was a continuing of the wonder-journey of life. To the peoples of the Idea the after-life is hell, or purgatory, or nothingness, and paradise is an inadequate fiction. (Ibid., p. 174)

The Escaped Cock is the best fictional expression of Lawrence's belief in the "wonder-journey of life." And both the novel and *Etruscan Places* see compulsion and fear as that which robs man of his insight into the splendor of a real religion of life. Both compulsion and imposition eventually kill the vital life spark.

So he went his way, and was alone. But the way of the world was past belief, as he saw the strange entanglement of passions and circumstance and compulsion everywhere, but always the dread insomnia of compulsion. It was fear, the ultimate fear of death, that made men mad. So always he must move on, for if he stayed, his neighbours wound the strangling of their fear and bullying round him. There was nothing he could touch, for all, in a mad assertion of the ego, wanted to put a compulsion on him, and violate his intrinsic solitude. It was the mania of individuals, it was the mania of cities and societies and hosts, to lay a compulsion upon a man, upon all men. For men and women alike were mad with the egoistic fear of their own nothingness. (*The Escaped Cock*, Part I)

140

Why has mankind had such a craving to be imposed upon? Why this lust after imposing creeds, imposing deeds, imposing buildings, imposing language, imposing works of art? The thing becomes an imposition and a weariness at last. Give us things that are alive and flexible, which won't last too long and become an obstruction and a weariness. (*Etruscan Places*, p. 123)

Etruscan Places is a book whose final effect on the reader is impossible to summarize. It is as much, if not more, about Lawrence as about the Etruscans, and it is the sheer delight which one takes in Lawrence's enthusiastic response to this ancient race which gives it its real power. That response is still alive on the page, and one can easily understand why Lawrence could return from the trip spiritually and creatively refreshed and encouraged. All of the influences and events we have been considering lead up to Lawrence's Etruscan trip, and having seen one undying, vibrant expression of a natural religion of life, of the resurrection, of a phallic consciousness, he was ready to write "The Escaped Cock," where the risen man returns and discovers with surprise "what an astonishing place the phenomenal world is. . . ." (CL, p. 975)

III. FROM STORY TO NOVEL

By 8 October 1928, Lawrence had sold "The Escaped Cock" to *The Forum*. Almost no critical attention has been given to this first version of Part I. Although the basic plot line is identical, there are several interesting variations in thematic images and also important differences in emphasis between the short story and novel versions.

The following two columns, one for the *Forum* text and one for the final text, are from exactly parallel points in the narrative, and a comparison will reveal developments and changes in emphasis. One must remember that the *Forum* text was published as a short story complete in itself (although Lawrence most likely already had the second half in mind), while the revised version of the same story was rewritten to be connected to the important Part II, the "phallic half" of the novel. In order to offer an additional means of comparison, I have grouped the material into three symbolic clusters, i.e., the cock, life, and the man who had died. This not only reveals how a short story was altered to form part of a novel, but it strongly suggests, I believe, a radical change in the visionary imagination and the motivating impetus of Lawrence. In short, the theme of "The Escaped Cock" is *not* the exact theme of Part I of *The Escaped Cock*.

THE *FORUM* TEXT	FINAL TEXT
(1) THE COCK	(1) THE COCK
a. cock's crow of—fiery clamor	a. cock's crow of—fiery colour
b. cock's crow—It was the assertion of life, the loud outcry of the cock's petty triumph in life.	b. cock's crow—It was the necessity to live, and even to cry out the triumph of life.
c. cock's crow—another challenge to all the world to deny his existence.	c. cock's crow—another challenge from life to death

(2) LIFE

a. The man who had died looked grimly on life and saw a vast assertiveness everywhere. . . .

b. . . . raging with insistence and with assertion.

c. He heard . . . their raging assertion of themselves

d. . . . the everlasting, self-assertive violence of life

e. . . . the raging ocean of life. And the rage of life seemed more fierce and compulsive to him even than the rage of death. The scythe-stroke of death was a shadow, compared to the raging upstarting of life, the determined turmoil of life. And this mad insistence of chaotic life, insisting against everything else, was repellent to the man who had died. He looked on, relieved that it was no longer his affair. At twilight. . .

(2) LIFE

a. The man who had died looked nakedly on to life, and saw a vast resoluteness everywhere. . . .

b. glowing with desire and with assertion

c. (omitted)

d. everlasting resoluteness of life

e. . . . the swaying ocean of life. And the destiny of life seemed more fierce and compulsive to him even than the destiny of death. The doom of death was a shadow, compared to the raging destiny of life, the determined surge of life. At twilight. . . .

(3) THE MAN WHO HAD DIED

a. "My triumph?" he asked. "But what was my triumph? I was killed in my mission and it is dead now to me. I can't come back. I am in another world, Madeleine, and not in touch with men. Yet still I am a man and still young. Is it not so? What will be the outcome, since now I am dead and risen, there is a gulf between me and all mankind? I am out of touch."

b. ". . . my mission is over, death has utterly cut it off from me. When a man dies, he rises in another world, even if there are the same faces. Death has put me far beyond even that salvation I dreamed of. Oh,

(3) THE MAN WHO HAD DIED

a. "My triumph," he said, "is that I am not dead. I have outlived my mission, and know no more of it. It is my triumph. I have survived the day and the death of my interference, and am still a man. I am young still, Madeleine, not even come to middle age. I am glad all that is over. It had to be. But now I am glad it is over, and the day of my interference is done. The teacher and the saviour are dead in me; now I can go about my own business, into my own single life."

b. ". . . my mission is over, and my teaching is finished, and death has saved me from my own salvation. Oh Madeleine, I want to take my single way in life, which is my portion. My public life is over, the life

142

Madeleine, I don't know what world I have risen to. But I have risen out of touch with the old. And now I wait for my Father to take me up again."

c. So he spoke a little, quiet word to her and turned away. He could not touch the little, personal body—the little, personal life—in this woman nor in any other. He turned away and abided by the greater ruling.

d. He had risen bodily from the dead, but what his body had come alive for he did not know. He only knew that he was bodily out of touch with mankind; he who had previously *held* himself out of touch, in his little life, now was beyond touch. He had no desire in him, save the desire that none should touch him.
The peasant came. . . .

e. "Now I belong to my Father, though I know not what he is, nor where he is. And still he is."
. . . He wondered what he should do, for it seemed strange to be in a world of men and women and to have no touch with them. He said to himself: "Why has the connection of touch gone out of me?"

f. "I cannot touch my fellow men because they smell of greed and fear. It is fear of death that hampers them. Why don't they die, to be rid of their staleness and their littleness, covered up as they are and gnawed by the weariness of their greed and the compulsion of their fear? But it is vain to speak."

of my conviction and my mission, the life of my self-importance. Now I can wait on life, and say nothing and have no one betray me.

c. . . . So he spoke a quiet, courteous word to her, and turned away.

d. Risen from the dead, he had realised at last that the body, too, has its little life, and beyond that, the greater life. . . . Now he knew that he had risen for the greater life of the body. . . . moving towards the living being with whom he could mingle his body. . . . there was time, an eternity of time. . . . And he knew how rare was the risen body, the twice-born limbs rare, rarer far than the twice-born spirit, which could house in greedy flesh.
The peasant came. . . .

e. Now I belong to no one, and have no connection, and my mission or gospel is gone from me.
. . . Whatever came of touch between himself and the race of man, henceforth, should come without trespass or compulsion. For he said to himself: I tried to compel them to live, so they compelled me to die. It is always so, with compulsion. The recoil kills the advance. Now is my time to be alone.

f. (omitted)

g. "I will wander the earth and say nothing; for strange is the phenomenal world, whose essential body is my Father. I will wander like an iris walking naked within the inner air, well within the Father, and I shall be in the outer air as well. I shall see all the noise and the dust, and smell the fear, and brush past the greed, and beware. But I will go with the Father around me, with my body erect and procreant within the inner air. Perhaps within the inner air I shall meet other men, perhaps women, and we shall be in touch. If not, it is no matter, for my movement and my uprising is within the Father, and I stand naked within him as the irises do. And he is all about me, and my whole body is procreant in him."

"And men will cake themselves up with my words also, till they are heavy with the caked mud thereof. So it is! And if they will not go into the bath, the deluge will fall on them. And some, no doubt, will rise out of the inner earth, which is the Father, like flowers upon the inner air, which is the Father the same. And from the Father under the earth to the Father over the earth, they will unfold their nakedness entire as the irises do that rise from the mud, glistening in the inner air."

g. I will wander the earth, and say nothing. For nothing is so marvellous as to be alone in the phenomenal world, which is raging and yet apart. And I have not seen it, I was too much blinded by my confusion within it. Now I will wander among the stirring of the phenomenal world, for it is the stirring of all things among themselves which leaves me purely alone.

It can be seen that the *Forum* text and the final version differ considerably in *emphasis*, and I believe that even thematically the two are quite distinct. By referring to another of Lawrence's stories, a suggestive pattern of development from the *Forum* text to *The Escaped Cock* can be pointed out. Keith Sagar dates the composition of the unfinished short story "The Man Who Was Through With The World" as 27 February—8 March 1927 (*The Art of D. H. Lawrence*, p. 171). This would place this story of Henry the hermit just prior to the Rozanov review and "The Escaped Cock." These two stories and *The Escaped Cock*, Part I, suggest a thematic progression. For example, as Sagar says,

> Henry the Hermit is very much a misanthropist. . . . Holiness evades him. . . . What he misses in the hermit life is a purpose. . . (pp. 176-177)

In "The Man Who Was Through With The World," Henry describes his feelings in the following manner:

144

He felt, however, a bit vague about God. In his youth he had been sent to Sunday School, but he had long been through with all that. He had, as a matter of fact, even forgotten the Lord's prayer, like the old man in the Tolstoi parable. If he tried to remember it, he mixed it up with The Lord is my Shepherd, and felt annoyed. He might, of course, have fetched himself a Bible. But he was through with all that. (*The Princess and Other Stories*, p. 149)

Henry obviously lacks any definite religious impulse; he loathes his fellow man; and as the story breaks off, it seems that he is totally without any intent in life—except to be a hermit.

The man who had died in *The Forum's* "The Escaped Cock" has developed some from this purely misanthropic and visionless stage. But everywhere around him, he finds the "everlasting self-assertion of life" (the word "assertion" is consistently omitted from the text of the two part novel) and like Henry, he finds life generally contemptible:

The outer air is dirty with fear; for all beasts, but especially man, sweat greed and fear till the atmosphere of men stinks. If they would but die, they would be so much cleaner on the air.

This man who had died wishes his fellow man to die into "the inner air," which he called "the Father." Unlike Henry, he has risen to a new life—but most assuredly not the new full life of the final version. In the *Forum* version, the man who had died is a bit bewildered at his resurrection, he fails completely to understand its meaning, and all he can resort to are numerous clichés: "But now I must ascend to my Father," and "Now may I stand within the Father." (It should be noted that successive manuscript drafts indicate that Lawrence attempted to alter "the Father" phrase in the final draft, and most of them were revised to a less strictly specific and orthodox phrase.) But even though he has some religious development beyond Henry the hermit, the first man who had died is by no means clear about "the Father" who appears so important to him: "Now I belong to my Father, though I know not what he is, nor where he is."

In addition to the differences in attitudes toward life (2a: "assertion" vs. "resoluteness") and the changes in the cock's "petty triumph in life" (1b), some other differences between the first and last published versions of Part I can be noted. The final man who had died is much surer of himself; he doesn't assume an almost ridiculous (satirical?) stance before Madeleine, asking such revealing frantic questions as "What will be the outcome, since now I am dead and risen. . . ?" In contrast, the final man who had died knows, perhaps intuitively, that his task is to "take my single way in life." Furthermore the first man who had died says that he must "wait for my Father to take me up again" while the final man who had died is quite content to "wait on life."

Furthermore, much of what the man who had died in the *Forum* text says *precludes* the possibility of an eventual union with the priestess of Isis in Part II.

He could not touch the little personal body—the little, personal life—in this woman nor in any other.

145

And later,

> And perhaps within *the Father* he could meet a woman erect and quite uncovered and encompassed *by the Father* as the iris is. Then they could put the difference of their nakedness together and not be disappointed. (Italics added)

Compare this near asceticism and uncertainty tinged with a stifling puritanism to the comparative surety of the final man who had died, a surety which is definitely sexual.

> And perhaps one evening, I shall meet a woman who can lure my risen body, yet leave me my aloneness.

Clearly Lawrence had to make numerous revisions in his first text of Part I. As I see the development of these three characters, Henry the hermit becomes the man who had died of the *Forum* text, a rather weak, foolish, and bewildered man. It is only with the man who had died of *The Escaped Cock* that we find the further evolution of a truly mystic new man, a man risen to a new life of beauty and purpose, and one who learns the invaluable power of the healing phallus. The Rozanov review fits in here, for Rozanov's work pointed out to Lawrence a valid attack on Christianity, and consequently, when I read the *Forum* text and then compare *The Escaped Cock*, I find in the former an almost satirical portrait of the Christ, similar to Rozanov's bitter satire. Zytaruk's thesis might thus be amended to note the influence of Rozanov on "The Escaped Cock" rather than on the novel.

One further interesting point can be made about the *Forum* appearance of "The Escaped Cock." As Lawrence's letter to Helen Bramble (17 April 1928; CL, p. 1057) indicates, there was a great public uproar over the story. The May 1928 issue of the magazine printed the following note by the editors: "No story ever published by *The Forum* has aroused so violent an outburst of contrary opinions as 'The Escaped Cock' by D. H. Lawrence in the February number." Apparently Lawrence was actually called a "traitor and enemy of the human race" by some irate reader, and he felt it necessary to caution Miss Bramble about any actions on the part of the *Forum* staff which might result from the fear of losing subscribers. We don't know exactly how disturbed the publishers and editors were, but with the recent discovery of a variant front cover for the February 1928 issue, now with a Mayan temple facade design and with the title of Lawrence's story altered to "Resurrection," it is very possible that they took some defensive action. Be that as it may, the contents of these two variants of the February issue, including the Table of Contents where the story is properly referred to as "The Escaped Cock," are identical; only the front cover has been changed. "Cock" may or may not have been an intentional pun on Lawrence's part in the title, but the possibility of its being judged so, and hence highly offensive to the readers of *The Forum* may have forced them to change the title to "Resurrection" on the front cover.

146

IV. DATING THE COMPOSITION OF PART II

After *The Forum* purchased "The Escaped Cock," Lawrence spent the fall of 1927 working on his *Collected Poems* and *Collected Stories*, both to be published by Secker. By November 1927, he had finally decided, after several months of indecision, that *Lady Chatterley's Lover* was to be published privately. He started work on the novel again, and he completed the third version in 1928.

In January 1928, Harry and Caresse Crosby, owners of The Black Sun Press in Paris, were on an Egyptian trip. Harry Crosby purchased a copy of Lawrence's *The Plumed Serpent* in Cairo and read it with great enthusiasm as they travelled up the Nile. Crosby evidently wrote to Lawrence at the first opportunity, for on 26 February 1928, Lawrence wrote his first letter to the Crosbys. In his letter he complimented Crosby on his admiration for the sun (Lawrence refers to the sun as "the real Ra"). Crosby's favorite color was black and, according to his wife, he "worshipped the sun"—hence the title of their press, and Lawrence also suggested that Crosby "dip [his] hand in Osiris." (It was also at this very time that Lawrence was reading a French book on Egypt which may have refreshed his acquaintance with the myth of Osiris to the point where he could utilize it in the yet unwritten Part II.) In the meantime, Lawrence was tentatively making arrangements for publication. On 6 March, he wrote to Brett that he was agreeable to the publication of "The Escaped Cock," by his old Taos friend, Willard "Spud" Johnson (apparently Johnson and/or Brett had read it in *The Forum*). He admits that he had thought of adding "perhaps another 5000 words. Of course I don't know if I could. I haven't yet seen the thing in print. . . ."

In April 1928 Lawrence made arrangements to write an "Introduction" for Harry Crosby's volume of poetry, *Chariot of the Sun*, and to send "Sun" to Crosby for publication. Other than these two literary pieces, Lawrence wrote little during this time, for he was very busy seeing *Lady Chatterley's Lover* through the press, and he did little additional work other than painting. It is therefore very unlikely that he started work on the second "phallic" half of *The Escaped Cock* before he left Italy and the Villa Mirenda for good on 10 June 1928.

Lawrence was not in good health at this time, having had a severe attack of what he called "influenza" in May, and he and Frieda left with the Brewsters for the more suitable climate of Grenoble, France. Here Lawrence was so ill that the hotel manager asked them to leave, for Lawrence's severe cough was disturbing and frightening the other guests. The Lawrences and the Brewsters then went to Chexbres-sur-Vevey, Switzerland, and it is in two letters written from here that we have the first mention of work on the second half of *The Escaped Cock*. It is difficult to tell exactly when Lawrence began it. He certainly had not by 6 March; he may have some time around 22 March when his letters contain frequent references to the "phallic consciousness" and mention the theories of Rozanov. The last months of the spring and early summer were certainly very crowded with his work on the proofs of *Lady Chatterley's Lover* and his painting. It should also be noted that his letters of 17 April to Miss Bramble and 3 June to Spud Johnson contain no mention of any work on the second half. Judging from these facts, it appears almost certain that Part II of *The Escaped Cock* was not started much before the arrival at Chexbres-sur-Vevey.

147

On 19 June, Frieda felt Lawrence had regained enough strength to be left alone, and she left Chexbres-sur-Vevey for Baden-Baden. On 21 June, Lawrence wrote Harry Crosby a short letter in which he casually mentioned that he was "doing a story with mixed suns in it: call down wrath on my poor head." This seems to alude to the first draft of Part II with its obvious "mixed suns":

> All this is lore of Isis, and the maid knew it. The lotus waits for a deeper sun. It will not open to the touch of the common sun alone. The day-sun dies, the moon arises, in the darkness a scattered sun invisibly assembles himself. And then the lotus rises on the flood, up-lifts, straightens her head, and expands, in the brilliant and many-pointed radiance of the glad womb.
> But not for the touch of the common sun. And not for the touch of the common sons of men. (MS. F, pp. 8-9)

In a letter apparently written on 24 June to Frieda, Lawrence says that he "worked over my Isis story a bit—am going to try it on Earl." From this it is apparent that Frieda knew what story he was referring to, so the preliminary stages at least were started *before* Frieda left on 19 June.

On 9 July, the Lawrences moved to Châlet Kesselmatte, Gsteig bei Gstaad, and Lawrence wrote and asked the Brewsters to join them. They did so on 11 July. Shortly thereafter Lawrence read to them the unfinished story written almost three years earlier, "The Flying Fish." The Brewsters offer a recollection of this in their memoir of Lawrence.

> One afternoon he sat holding a child's copybook saying that he was going to read us an unfinished novel he had started on the way back from Mexico when he was very ill, and written down by Frieda from his dictation. It was called "The Flying Fish" with the old haunting symbolisms of *pisces*.
> As he read, it seemed to reach an ever higher more serene beauty. Suddenly he stopped saying:
> "The last part will be regenerate man, a real life in this Garden of Eden."
> We asked: "What shall you make him do? What will he be like, the regenerate man, fulfilling life on earth?"
> "I don't just know."
> The enduring beauty of "The Flying Fish" made us ask at various times if he had not finished it, to which he would reply, that we must not urge him to finish it. "I've an intuition I shall not finish that novel. It was written so near the borderline of death, that I never have been able to carry it through, in the cold light of day." (Brewster, p. 288)

This has several implications: Lawrence believed that completion of the story would involve a regenerate man, which may be, but doesn't have to be the "resurrected man" of The Escaped Cock; secondly, at this reading, Lawrence did not know what the regenerate man would be like—it is, therefore, almost certain that he had not *completed* the final draft of Part II; and perhaps most important for our purposes, at a time when we know with certainty that Lawrence was working on The Escaped Cock, he was also thinking about "The Flying Fish," and as was pointed out earlier, much of the "greater day" imagery of that short story is found in the completed novel.

It would seem likely, from the 20 July letter to Brett, that Lawrence had started and completed Part II of *The Escaped Cock* sometime between 19 June and 20 July, for in this letter he tells Dorothy Brett, "And I haven't given Crosby Gaige the second half of *Escaped Cock*, though I've written it, & think it's lovely. But somehow I don't want to let it go out of my hands." (Letter V above) The time between 20 July and 28 August was probably taken up with rewriting Part I. The letter to Aldous and Maria Huxley of 31 July, for example, contains some lines which seem to indicate this:

> Well, I feel there's not much of me left. What little there is gives you the Easter Kiss and hopes we'll crow in chorus once more, one day, like risen Easter eggs. (CL, p. 1072)

Lawrence's method of composition of *The Escaped Cock* was a variation on his habit of writing and rewriting a novel several times. From an examination of Manuscript B, and a comparison of it with Manuscript A and with the *Forum* text of Part I, it seems evident that Lawrence had the latter before him and was revising it as he typed out a final draft of Part I (MS. C). Furthermore, MS. B, typed by Lawrence, has an ending identical to the ending of the *Forum* text, *except* for the last paragraph which is Lawrence's handwritten addition. Thus this manuscript of Part I, the manuscript which was sent to Enid Hilton for typing and the text of which was used for The Black Sun Press edition, is at least two revision stages farther along than the *Forum* text, one during typing and the other later.

By 27 August, Lawrence had completed his work on the novel, and he wrote to Pollinger: "I finished the second half of *The Escaped Cock*, about 10,000 words—rather lovely—but I feel tender about giving it out for publication—as I felt tender about *Lady C*. . . . And this story is one of my thin-skinned ones." (CL, p. 1081) But Lawrence was apparently very quick about making up his mind, for in a letter apparently written on the next day (Letter VI above), he asked Enid Hilton to type the manuscript for him, and he sent it to her—a typescript of Part I and holograph of Part II—on 2 September 1928. (Huxley, p. 750)

V. PUBLICATION: THE NOVEL AND THE WATERCOLOR DECORATIONS

Lawrence's plans for the publication of *The Escaped Cock* changed several times. On 6 March 1928, Lawrence had informed Dorothy Brett that Willard Johnson might print Part I (probably the *Forum* text) on his private press in Taos, but little more than a week later he wrote his agent Curtis Brown (15 March 1928):

> Thanks for yours about Gaige. I thought that was gone—forgotten— so when Willard Johnson—the boy who did that *Laughing Horse* number of me in Santa Fé—wrote and asked me if he could do that story on his little press in Taos, I said "yes." He hasn't got a bean—so there's no money there. But I told him if he got ahead to fix up with

149

the New York office. But perhaps he won't do it. If he doesn't, I shall write a second half to it—the phallic second half I always intended to add to it—and send it to you for Gaige to look at. Otherwise later I'll write a 10,000-word thing and send it. It's a length I like—and I hate having to fit magazines. (Huxley, p. 709)

And apparently preliminary arrangements at least were made with the Crosby Gaige firm, for Lawrence wrote Johnson on 3 June,

don't print *The Escaped Cock* as my agents say Crosby Gaige will put it in his privately-printed list & give me $1000. If he will, so much the better, & I can give you something else, if you like. (Letter IV, above)

Meanwhile Lawrence was busy writing Part II. And when this was completed and the typescripts received from Enid Hilton, he became very careful about *any* publication of what was now a short novel in two parts. He sent one copy of the typescript to Crosby Gaige in October and by 7 January 1929 some decision had been made by the American firm. He wrote to Curtis Brown on that date:

All right, let the Gaige people do the first part of *Escaped Cock* if they want to, but the second half of the story is the best. So please put in a clause that I can reprint their half in six months' time, because I shall put out the whole story because I know it is good and I believe in it. If I let the first half go now alone, it is because it has already appeared, and it will make way for the second. (Huxley, p. 778)

And on 2 March 1929, he wrote to Orioli:

The Crosby Gaige man drew up a contract for the first half of *Escaped Cock*—in which I promise not to issue the second half till 1930. But I wrote back saying he must put in a clause: that the title must be *The Escaped Cock. Part One*—and that at the end he must put: *Here ends the First Part of the Escaped Cock.*—That puts salt on *his* tail. He's hanging fire—not answered yet. If he backs out, I don't care— then we'll do the whole thing for Easter 1930—it would just make a nice book for you to do, about sixty pages. (Letter VIII, above)

But publication by Orioli was not to materialize, for the Lawrences met with Harry and Caresse Crosby in Paris during the next month and made arrangements for publication by the Crosbys' Black Sun Press. Lawrence apparently had at least part of one of the typescripts with him at the Paris meeting, for the correspondence between Lawrence and the Crosbys indicates that this was their first knowledge of the story and Lawrence therefore had to leave the typescript with them for their more careful consideration. It was not until some months later that Lawrence was absolutely assured that the Crosbys would follow through with their first enthusiasm for the story and print it. On 2 August 1929 he wrote to ask them if they had "got cold feet about *The Escaped Cock*, since the ridiculous fuss over my pictures. . . ." The Crosbys had not written Lawrence in some time, and he was anxious for a definite commitment:

150

And I want to tell you not to bother for a moment about the thing, if you don't want to. If circumstances have so worked that it makes it inconvenient for you to publish the story, will you only please let me have back the MSS.—you have all my copies—so that I can make other arrangements. Believe me, I shall understand perfectly, if you tell me your plans are changed. (Huxley, p. 813)

The Crosbys finally answered and arrangements were made. The decorations were started by 8 August, and by 15 August Lawrence had sent them and the corrected proofs off to Caresse Crosby.

The decorations consist of a frontispiece (reproduced on the cover of this edition) and a head- and tail-piece each for Part I and Part II. The frontispiece, reduced in size from the original, is a sketch of two figures, obviously the priestess of Isis in her yellow robe and the naked man who had died. She is facing him, leaning forward, and both hands appear to be intent on "the death-wound through his belly." He is arched away from her, appearing both to resist and to yield to her efforts to heal him. Between them is a shallow incense burner or "brazier," and up from this leaps a long tongue of flame, occupying exactly the area between the two figures. ("For here again he felt desperate, faced by the demand of life, and burdened still by his death. . . . She was stooping now, looking at the scar in the soft flesh of the socket of his side, a scar deep and like an eye with endless weeping, just in the soft socket above the hip. It was here that his blood had left him, and his essential seed.") The face of the blonde priestess looking down at the wound is hidden from view, but the face of the man, although very faintly drawn, has the same outlines as that of the risen man in Lawrence's painting "Resurrection"—the face of Lawrence. The two figures are placed against a background of large swirls of greens, yellows, reds, and browns, suggesting a highly symbolic kind of cosmic setting, as if the figures were acting out a timeless rite of immense importance.

The much smaller head-piece for Part I is circular and in a blood red with two shades of green. The figure is that of a cock in full flight escaping from a grasping hand of a man. The tail-piece for Part I is a vivid red flower—perhaps a lily or a poppy anemone—suggesting spring and resurrection. The head-piece for Part II is again circular and again in reds and greens. There is a figure of a woman, the priestess of Isis, head bowed and holding in her hand an ankh, the ancient Egyptian symbol of life. Since she is alone, and since there is a certain sadness in the muted green of her figure, we can assume that this is a portrayal of "Isis in Search." There are swirling patterns, as in the frontispiece, and they are suggestive perhaps of the infinite flux of life. There are also two other ankhs in the background. The tail-piece at the end of Part II is a fitting pictorial closing for the novel, for it is of three red acorns, the seeds of a new life, and a green leaf. (See the last paragraph of the novel: "I sowed the seed of my life and my resurrection. . . .") The man who had died has sown the seed of a new kind of life, the woman of Isis is to bear his child, and the novel can end—"So let the boat carry me. Tomorrow is another day."

Lawrence was never very satisfied with the business end of his relationship with the Black Sun Press. He was from the beginning extremely concerned with securing proper copyright in America and Europe. (There had been several pirated editions of *Lady Chatterley's Lover* the previous year and Lawrence felt that he had lost a great deal of money.) He was extremely unhappy that Caresse had arbitrarily decided to send the entire edition to America, and as early as 8 August (Letter XV, above), apparently just after he received a definite commitment from the Crosbys, he was discussing the possibility of a public edition for England. On 15 October Lawrence wrote to Mrs. Crosby:

> I am having the book set up in London—no decorations—just an ordinary unlimited edition, at, perhaps, 7/6. But I shan't release it till March or April, unless there is a private appearance. (Letter XXVII, above)

This was mostly a kind of bluffing rearguard action on the part of Lawrence, for Lahr (as Lawrence's late letters to him indicate) had neither a copy nor a set of proofs to set type from. Lawrence means, I think, that he is *going to* have an English public edition. (Lahr did not receive a copy of the text until late November. See unpublished letter 62 in list.) In the meantime, Lawrence's health was getting very bad. He wrote to Lahr (24 January 1930):

> I haven't written—been so seedy—now the doctor says I must lie quite still, do no work at all, see nobody, & try to get better—not even think of work. So I am obeying.
> I have no further news of the Hahn: shall let you know. What was your idea about it? To do a public edition, with another title? Tell me. (Letter XXIX, above)

And apparently this was what Lahr had in mind, for on 3 February 1930, a very ill Lawrence, now in a sanatorium and with less than three weeks to live, wrote Lahr that *The Man Who Had Died* was an acceptable title. (CL, p. 1240) Lahr probably suggested it. The frequency of inaccuracies in the texts of some of Lawrence's novels is common knowledge, but in this instance, one can say with certainty that none of the editions since the Black Sun Press edition have been published with a proper *title*. Lawrence clearly said in one of his last letters (Letter XXXI, above) that *The Man Who Had Died*, not the title which has been used in all printings since 1929—*The Man Who Died*—was an acceptable alternate title. Nor have any editions subsequent to the Crosbys' carried the title (or subtitle) *The Escaped Cock*. Lawrence insisted on *The Escaped Cock* appearing at least as a subtitle.

VI. THE FINAL STATEMENT

We have seen that Lawrence's review of one Russian critic of Christianity was done contemporaneously with the *Forum* text. Shortly before he died, and at a time when he was working on the details of a public edition of his completed resurrection story, Lawrence wrote an "Introduction" to *The Grand Inquisitor*, translated by S. S. Koteliansky. (See *The Quest for Rananim*, letters of 9 January, and 25 January 1930.) In this piece Lawrence recalls his earlier reading (1913) of *The Grand Inquisitor* and compares his present reaction.

> I still see a trifle of cynical-satanical showing-off. But under that I hear the final and unanswerable criticism of Christ. And it is a deadly, devastating summing-up, unanswerable because borne out by the long

experience of humanity. It is reality versus illusion, and the illusion was Jesus', while time itself retorts with the reality. (*Phoenix*, p. 283)

Lawrence feels that men demand "miracle, mystery, and authority," that Christianity fails to provide men with these essentials, and that it "is too difficult for men, the vast mass of men." Christianity is the impossible "ideal." In summing up his reaction to Dostoievsky's story, Lawrence reiterates much of the thought of *The Escaped Cock:*

> The earthly bread is leavened with the heavenly bread. The heavenly bread is life, is contact, and is consciousness. In sowing the seed man has his contact with earth, with sun and rain: and he *must not* break the contact. In the awareness of the springing of the corn he has his ever-renewed consciousness of miracle, wonder, and mystery: the wonder of creation, procreation, and re-creation, following the mystery of death and the cold grave. It is the grief of Holy Week and the delight of Easter Sunday. And man must not, must not lose this supreme state of consciousness out of himself, or he has lost the best part of him. Again, the reaping and the harvest are another contact, with earth and sun, a rich touch of the cosmos, a living stream of activity, and then the contact with harvesters, and the joy of harvest-home. All this is life, life, it is the heavenly bread which we eat in the course of getting the earthly bread. (*Phoenix*, p. 289)

All of his life Lawrence was concerned with the thought contained in that phrase he wrote shortly before he died, and it is the central point of his last great novel: man "*must not* break the contact" with his "ever-renewed consciousness of miracle, wonder, and mystery: the wonder of creation, procreation, and re-creation, following the mystery of death and the cold grave. It is the grief of Holy Week and the delight of Easter Sunday."

VII. THE MANUSCRIPTS

Eight different manuscripts are known to have survived. They are as follows:

PART I

A.) AMS, Iowa State Education Association, Notebook, pp. 1-22.
This is actually only a sketch of Part I. It is furthermore difficult to determine with certainty whether this is a rough draft for the *Forum* story, "The Escaped Cock," or a later completely rewritten version of Part I of what eventually became the novel *The Escaped Cock* in two parts. It is, however, almost certain that this is the original draft of Part I, and the *Forum* Text and all subsequent texts of Part I probably are revised and expanded from this one. For our purposes, it has been considered only as a preliminary sketch.

B.) TMS, Private collection, pp. 1-25. See Tedlock p. 65 for description.
This typescript, corrected and revised by Lawrence, matches the text of the

Forum version of Part I except for variations in punctuation and spelling, and the omission from the *Forum* text of the .final sentence added in Lawrence's hand:

> For the inner air is always within it, and out of the dust one can look at the freshness which is the Father, wherein the Iris unfolds himself, and wherein my young cock has his kingdom, sometimes.

C.) TMS, heavily corrected in Lawrence's hand, the University of Texas at Austin, pp. 1-22, uncatalogued.
This manuscript was almost certainly the one which Lawrence said he typed himself (Letter 34). In some places the text is *close* to the *Forum* text, but it is actually a new manuscript, a manuscript prepared to connect with Part II and obviously made for the novel. This is the manuscript (along with holograph MS. G of Part II) which Lawrence sent to Enid Hilton to be typed (Letter 21).

D.) TMS, The University of Texas at Austin, pp. 1-32, Farmer A8.
Lightly corrected, but only in those instances in which it varies from MS. C (see above). Most of this manuscript is a carbon of MS. E. The corrections were made by the typist, Mrs. Enid Hilton. This manuscript was used by the type-setter for the preparation of the Black Sun Press edition and was never corrected or revised by Lawrence. (See discussion below in Section VIII.)

E.) TMS, The University of Texas at Austin, pp. 1-32, Farmer A7.
This original typescript is marked with "corrections" (by Mrs. Hilton) as was MS. D, but it also has *additional* significant revisions and alterations in Lawrence's hand which have not been previously published. This is the manuscript used for the present text. MSS. D, E, and H (below) are typed on the same watermarked ("Silver Cross") paper.

PART II

F.) AMS, holograph rough sketch of Part II, incomplete, University of Californit at Berkeley (only a typed copy of the original holograph copy). See Tedlock, pp. 66-69, for description. Original holograph in private collection. Pages 1-22.
Almost certainly the first draft of Part II. The Commentary quotes from significant passages of this manuscript.

G.) AMS, Iowa State Education Association, Notebook (containing also MS. A), pp. 1-49.
This is the original draft of the complete Part II; it is a holograph manuscript in Lawrence's hand with extensive interlinear revision in some sections. This manuscript was mailed to Enid Hilton (along with MS. C) for typing.

H.) TMS, The University of Texas at Austin, pp. 33-71, uncatalogued.
Typescript prepared from MS. G by Enid Hilton on "Silver Cross" water-

marked paper. Corrections and revisions in Lawrence's hand; otherwise identical to MS. G, except for typing errors and attempts at a standardization of the punctuation of the dialogue and interior monologues. (See note below.) Various manuscript evidence indicates that this was used for the preparation of the Black Sun Press edition. But several passages, still extant in the manuscript, were unexplainably deleted from this edition. They have been restored in the present volume which follows this manuscript. (See Section VIII.)

Note: MSS. E and H, the manuscripts used for this edition, have been collated with MSS. C and G respectively. In other words, a comparison has been made between Lawrence's original manuscripts and the typist's copy. In those instances in which the paragraphing, spelling, or punctuation has been altered by the typist in E or H, the original format of C or G has been restored. The only liberties taken with the manuscripts used for the present edition were to employ, for the sake of consistency, Lawrence's original forms of interior monologue and dialogue. In all other instances Lawrence's text has been the final authority.

There is a complete typescript of *The Escaped Cock* in the University of New Mexico Library. This manuscript, however, bears no indication that Lawrence was ever involved in its composition. The few handwritten corrections are not in Lawrence's hand. Rather they appear to be in Frieda's handwriting, and a good guess might be that this text was used for one of the 1931 editions of the novel. It has the stamp of Curtis Brown's office on it. This manuscript is extraneous to the present study, and I will not refer to it in my discussions.

PAGE PROOFS:

Copy 1. The University of California at Los Angeles.
Copy 2. The University of Texas at Austin.
Copy 1 and copy 2 are identical textually, are identical page proofs. The corrections involve minor changes such as punctuation, spelling, and occasionally a word. The text of both sets of page proofs is otherwise identical to the Black Sun Press edition and does not contain the material in MSS. E or H. These page proofs do not, however, have identical corrections. For example, an error corrected in one may not be corrected in the other. The use of both is therefore necessary for a textual study.

VIII. THE TEXT

The principal editions of *The Escaped Cock*—those from The Black Sun Press, Secker, Knopf, and Heinemann—are substantially identical, differing primarily in punctuation. But if one goes to the manuscripts of the novel, one becomes aware of important variant readings and discovers that the published texts fail to include some of Lawrence's revisions and (in the case of Part II) some of the actual text. An investigation of all the available materials—manuscripts, letters, page proofs, etc.—is therefore desirable.

I begin with a summary statement of my conclusions: (1) No previous text of the novel can be regarded as entirely satisfactory in regard to (a) title, (b) punctuation and format, and (c) text. (2) While the present text may not be conclusively definitive (for reasons to be explained below), it comes closer to that ideal than any earlier edition. As for the evidence leading to these conclusions, first I shall collect the information available in the letters and try to ascertain which manuscripts were used by the Crosbys in printing their edition, and following that I shall discuss the text of the various manuscripts themselves.

The evidence of the letters is best presented in abbreviated form. My conjectures are indicated by brackets; they are based on a study of the manuscripts as listed in the preceding section of the Commentary and on the information in specific letters noted to the right of each entry. Numbers refer to the list of relevant Lawrence letters (see Appendix above, following the Letters); those printed in the present volume are asterisked.

1) Lawrence sent manuscript [MS. C, Part I and MS. G, Part II] to Enid Hilton . . . . 2 September 1928, Letter 21
2) Lawrence received typescripts [MS. E, Part I and MS. H, Part II, and one carbon copy, unidentified, hereafter referred to as TccMS]. Enid Hilton retains the original manuscripts which Lawrence sent her [MSS. C and G] . . . . 27 October 1928, Letter 22
3) Lawrence sent manuscript [TccMS] "to America," that is, to Crosby Gaige, at least by . . . . 27 October 1928, Letter 24
4) Lawrence asked Pollinger to "get the manuscript" [unidentified but see discussion below] . . . . 7 January 1929, Letter 26
5) Lawrence made arrangements during the Easter weekend 1929 to have the novel published by the Crosbys' Black Sun Press. He believed later that his agent in London, Curtis Brown, would send the Crosbys "the other copy of *Escaped Cock.*" [TccMS] . . . . 18 April 1929, Letter 30*
6) Curtis Brown has not sent the manuscript . . . . . 17 May 1929, Letter 31*
7) Lawrence discovered that he had only given "the second half" to the Crosbys. Lawrence sent AMS, Part I [MS. A] and has requested Enid Hilton to send manuscripts [MSS. C and G] . . 20 May 1929, Letters 32* & 33
8) Enid Hilton sent manuscripts [C and G] to Crosbys . . . .
                    7 June 1929, Enid Hilton to Caresse Crosby*
9) Lawrence assumed that Crosbys had received all the requested manuscripts [A, C, G, and TccMS] . . . . 7 June 1929, Letter 34*

What is the manuscript mentioned in 4)? The issue is complicated by the bipartite nature of the novel—thus we have two separate halves of a manuscript to account for. And it becomes even more complex: Mrs. Hilton tells me that she typed not one, but *two* carbons. We now have three possible typescripts—excluding Lawrence's own typescript, which is clearly MS. C.

Part I		Part II	
Original	E	H	
1st carbon	D or X	X	
2nd carbon	X or D	X	TccMS

Either the first or the second carbon could be the TccMS mentioned in 2), 3), 5), and 9), but one of the carbons has to include MS. D. (Manuscripts which appear not to have survived and of which there is no record are identified as "X.")

156

The manuscript in 4) therefore could have been a second carbon typescript of the novel still at that time in the possession of Enid Hilton in London. Lawrence would on occasion ask Pollinger to get copies of *Lady Chatterley's Lover* for distribution. A visit to Enid Hilton who was keeping several copies on hand would be possible, even likely, and Pollinger *could* have picked up a manuscript from her.

Mrs. Hilton informs me in letters of 9 January 1972 and 24 March 1973 that she had a second carbon: "As far as my memory serves, the third carbon [that is, the third copy, or the second carbon] was later sent to Lawrence or to the publisher" (9 January 1972), and the second carbon "was very poor, I remember, and may later have been thrown away." (24 March 1973). Mr. Pollinger tells me in a letter of 19 February 1973 that he does not "recall picking up the typescript of *The Escaped Cock* from anyone." From the evidence available, I am of the opinion that Mrs. Hilton was probably correct in her suggestion that the second carbon was thrown away. Lawrence had not requested a second carbon copy, and apparently Mrs. Hilton made it for her own reading copy. She has told me that she furthermore made a "hand-written copy" for herself. This would not have been necessary if the second carbon had been suitable; it was, however, "very poor." Also *neither* Mr. Pollinger *nor* Mrs. Hilton recalls an occasion when Mr. Pollinger obtained a manuscript from Mrs. Hilton. And none of Lawrence's letters indicate a knowledge of another carbon. Thus it would appear that the second carbon can be eliminated, reducing the possibilities to the following (all of these except MS. E will *eventually* be in the possession of the Crosbys):

	Part I		Part II
Original	E		H
1st carbon	D		X—TccMS

The manuscript of *The Escaped Cock* in 4) thus has to be one of the following:

1) As the letters indicate, Crosby Gaige was willing to publish only Part I, and Lawrence may have been asking Pollinger to get only Part II [MS. X, from TccMS] from Crosby Gaige.
2) Lawrence may have requested Pollinger to get, *at some future time*, the complete typescript [TccMS] from Crosby Gaige.
   I am excluding the original typescript for the following reasons. First, as 7) makes clear, Lawrence did not personally give the Crosbys a typescript of Part I. What copy of Part I the Crosbys later obtained had to originate from Curtis Brown. Second, as the discussion below of the actual manuscripts demonstrates, the Crosbys got and used MS. D, a carbon typescript.

As late as 2 March 1929, Lawrence indicates that he was waiting to hear a decision from Crosby Gaige, but by 31 March (Letter 27*) he had made tentative arrangements with the Crosbys to publish *both* parts of the novel. Any agreement with Crosby Gaige would certainly have then been superseded, and he would, under normal circumstances, have been obliged to return the manuscript to Lawrence's agent in London.

The existing correspondence between Lawrence and the Crosbys strongly suggests that they had not seen a complete manuscript of the novel before they met Lawrence in Paris. They might, of course, have read the early version of

Part I in *The Forum*, or Harry Crosby, who had earlier enthusiastically published an unexpurgated text of *Sun*, might have been interested in Lawrence's June 1928 reference to a new story with "mixed suns." At any rate, Lawrence clearly had to have some manuscript (either the complete novel, MSS. E and H, or Part II only, MS. H) with him when he met the Crosbys during Easter 1929. The Crosbys, however, clearly left Paris with only a manuscript of Part II [MS. H], and they requested a complete manuscript from Lawrence (Letter 32*). Lawrence informed Curtis Brown of this and asked them to forward one; therefore, they must now have had TccMS in their possession.

When he received the Crosbys' request, Lawrence also sent them MS. A, Part I, and asked Enid Hilton to send MSS. C, Part I and G, Part II. In the meantime, the Crosbys were to continue trying to get a manuscript from Curtis Brown's office. Lawrence assumes, by 7 June 1929, that they have received all of the following manuscripts:

> Part I
>> A—from Lawrence
>> C—from Enid Hilton
>> D—from Curtis Brown, Part I of TccMS
>
> Part II
>> G—from Enid Hilton
>> H—given to the Crosbys in Paris by Lawrence
>> X—Part II of TccMS from Curtis Brown

Of these, A and G are holograph drafts, while C is obviously an early draft with extensive interlinear revisions and additions. It would thus have been eliminated for possible typesetting use, and the Crosbys would then have the following typescripts to consider:

Part 1		Part II
Original	(none)	H
1st carbon	D	X=TccMS

The only unsatisfactory aspect of this conjecture is that the first carbon (D) bears no revisions or corrections (as does E of Part I), and Lawrence thus appears to have sent the manuscript (TccMS) to Crosby Gaige without having made any revisions, as he did in the original typescripts, MSS. E and H. This evident lack of careful concern for TccMS might be explained by Lawrence's frequent expression of small enthusiasm for the Crosby Gaige contract (see Letters 25 and 27*). MS. E, the original typescript of Part I, was the copy which Lawrence had intended to give, along with MS. H, to the Crosbys, but Letter 32* shows he had not done so. Thus MS. D, assuming as we are that the second carbon was thrown away, would be the text for Part I of the Crosbys' edition. Also we can now establish MS. H as the manuscript of Part II, for the Crosbys would have been immediately aware that it contained an obvious revision stage (Lawrence did not revise TccMS) beyond the unidentified carbon typescript of Part II also in their possession. The Black Sun Press edition was therefore printed from MS. D and MS. H, as the survey from the letters might suggest—and which is furthermore verified by an examination of the individual manuscripts.

I will now consider MSS. D and H separately, for each presents unique problems. The following should also make clear why it was necessary to explain in detail my reasons for believing that they were used by the Crosbys to set type.

MSS. D and E are almost identical textually to C—but there are three important areas in which D and E differ. First, as we mentioned in the note on the manuscripts (Commentary, Section VII), the original form of interior monologue and dialogue found in Lawrence's own typescript [MS. C] has been varied by the typist. For example,

MS. C, LAWRENCE'S ORIGINAL MANUSCRIPT	MS. D, TYPESCRIPT
Dialogue	

1. They believed him at once, yet the fear did not leave them. And they said:
    "Stay, Master. . . ." (MS p. 8)
	They believed him at once, yet fear did not leave them. And they said,
	    "Stay, Master. . . ." (MS pp. 10-11)
	
	MS. E restores colon.

2. So he said to the woman: "I would lie in the yard." And she swept. . . . (MS p. 9)	So he said to the woman, "I would lie in the yard." And she swept. . . . (MS p. 11) MS. E corrected comma to original colon.

3. And the man smiled, and held the bird dear, and he said to it: Surely thou art risen to the	And the man smiled and held his bird dear, and he said to it:
	    "Surely thou are risen. . . ."
	              (MS p. 24)
	
	As in MS. E and Black Sun Press, p. 31.

4. They answered suspiciously: "Why ask you of him?" (MS p. 21)	They answered suspiciously: "Why ask you of him?" (MS p. 29) As in MS. E and Black Sun Press, p. 39.
Interior monologue	

5. He felt her glance, and said to himself: Now my own followers will want to do me to death again. . . . (MS p. 14)	He felt her glance, and said to himself:"
	    "Now my own followers will want to do me to death again. . . ."
	              (MS p. 19)
	
	As in MS. E and Black Sun Press, p. 25, except superfluous quotation

mark removed from E.

6.   "But now I must ascend to my Father," he said, and he drew back, into the bushes, and so turned quickly and went away, saying to himself: Now I belong to no one, and have no connection, and mission or gospel is gone from me.   (MS p. 18)

"But now I must ascend to my father," he said, and he drew back into the bushes, and so turned quickly, and went away, saying to himself: "Now I belong to no one, and have no connection, and mission or gospel is gone from me." (MS p. 25)

As in MS. E and Black Sun Press, p. 33, except E *adds* "my" before "mission."

7. Then he said to himself: I will wander the earth. . . .   (MS p. 19)

Then he said to himself: "I will wander the earth. . . ."   (MS p. 26)

As in MS. E and Black Sun Press, p. 35, except Black Sun Press has semicolon instead of colon.

The above illustrates how the form of the interior monologue was usually, but not consistently, changed by the typist to resemble regular dialogue, whereas Lawrence's usual form (he is occasionally inconsistent) is to have no quotation marks and no new paragraph. (The present text follows this form, even in the few instances in which it varies from MS. C, Lawrence's typescript.)

Secondly, both typescripts—D and E—contain numerous handwritten corrections by the typist to make them correspond in instances of phrases and punctuation to C, but some of these corrections were made only on the original (E) and not on the carbon (D)—as 1, 2, and 5 above illustrate.

A third variation concerns the revisions and additions which Lawrence made on MS. E, but not on D. For examples of this, the reader is referred to the listing of variants. Thus, as intended by the author, MS. E is again the most accurate text, and all future printings should be based on this manuscript.

Now that we have established MS. E as the best text for Part I, we should also consider briefly the evidence which demonstrates that Ms. D was used for the first edition. Some errors in the listing above suggest this: for example, no. 5 which can still be found in the published text. Also the following errors are in MS. D, reappear in page proofs, and are corrected there:

1) And the man who had died, watched [instrusive comma]
2) For my reahh ends in my finger-tips [misspelling]
3) "Oh, Master!" And is it truly mine?" [superfluous quotation marks]

Secondly there are numerous typesetter's markings and even specific directions to the typesetter on page one of the text:

Format Sentimental / 24 lignes à la page / 12 Navion [?] plein

From all indications, MS D—not the other typescripts, C & E—was used for the Black Sun Press edition.

160

Since MS. E, the text used for the present edition of *The Escaped Cock*, is one revision stage beyond MS. D, it is obviously the correct text for Part I of any definitive edition. Establishing MS. H as the proper text for Part II, however, is more difficult. There is enough evidence to suggest that it was the text used by the Black Sun Press and that it was also the manuscript which Lawrence intended to be used. But a rather mysterious problem arises when we try to offer an explanation for the omitted passages. (See Table of Variants in the next section.) I shall first discuss the evidence which leads me to believe that MS. H was indeed the text used by the typesetter and then the problem of omissions.

MS. H is a fairly accurate typescript of MS. G—Lawrence's holograph manuscript of Part II which he sent to Enid Hilton for typing. Although this manuscript, like MSS. D and E, has been corrected by the typist, there are again certain areas in which the typescript is inaccurate. First, the incorrect and inconsistent formats for interior monologues and dialogues. Secondly, there are several other types of punctuation variants. Thirdly, there are further revisions by Lawrence which take this manuscript a composition stage beyond MS. G. All of these fall into much the same pattern as the discrepancies between the original and the typescript which I discussed in regard to Part I. But the most important new discovery we make when we compare MS. H with both page proofs and the published text is that several phrases extant in the manuscript have been inexplicably omitted from all printed forms of the text. These omissions are not corrections by Lawrence. If they were, one could easily conjecture that Lawrence made them *after* the September 1929 printing by the Black Sun Press. What is first necessary, therefore, is to examine MS. H and try to prove that it was the actual typescript used to set type.

MS. H does not have the tell-tale directions to the typesetter on the beginning page, as does D. However, there are a number of indications which suggest that it was used by the Crosbys' printer. Here are a few examples:

page, MS. H   *Evidence*

37 ff.   a. typesetter's markings—these are similar to those beginning at the end of MS. D.
                 b. a revision by Lawrence: that is, a revision stage beyond MS. G
                    When she was young. . . .   G
                    When she was young the girl. . . .   H

38   error in format of "dialogue" (in the context of the novel it is not actually dialogue and Lawrence does not treat it as such in MS. G.)
                    But he said to her:
                    "I have sacrificed. . . ."   H
                    But he said to her: I have sacrificed. . . . G

39   a. ". . . when the sun leans towards her to caress her.". . . . MS. H
                    The error of the four periods following the quotation reappears in the page proofs and is corrected there. In MS. G, Lawrence wrote
                    ". . . when the sun leans towards her to caress her."—
                    And the big. . . .

161

b. incorrect paragraphing, identical to error on p. 38

42   At Lenght. . . .
This misspelling reappears in the page proofs and is corrected there

46   the ir/revoc/able
Slash marks in the text indicating the division of the word. This word is divided in page proofs and in published Black Sun Press text.

66   This page is especially interesting, as it contains one of the omitted passages—a short undeleted and unmarked paragraph. (See Table of Variants, Part II, #49). The same page has the following error which reappears in corrected page proofs:
. . . have tender goddesses".

67   a. con/sum/mate
Slash marks indicating division of word
divided in page proofs
b. Two errors in typescript reappearing in page proofs

68-71   Each page has at least one error which reappears in page proofs

With the exception of the omitted phrases and some minor variants in spelling and punctuation, MS. H is identical to the page proofs of the novel. This fact, together with the evidence cited above—that is, typesetter's markings, indications of word divisions, and errors in the typescript which reappear in page proofs—suggests to me that MS. H was used by the typesetter for the Black Sun Press edition. It could perhaps be argued that some carbon typescript—MS. X, for example—could have been used and the omitted phrases clearly deleted there, by Lawrence or someone else. But such a conjecture would ignore such evidence as the dark ink stains on several pages of the manuscript, the word divisions, the typesetter's markings, and Lawrence's own revisions, all of which are present in MS. H. MS. D, a carbon of E, was not revised or corrected by Lawrence, as we have seen above. Following this pattern, it is unlikely that Lawrence would make any revisions on the carbon typescript of Part II only.

Even if we accept that MS. H was used by the typesetter, our primary problem with deciding upon the authenticity of all of it still confronts us. How do we account for the omissions listed in the Table of Variants, Part II? From all of the evidence and comment I can gather, it appears that any kind of censorship or editing of the text would be something which the Crosbys were not accustomed to doing under ordinary circumstances. On the other hand, these were not normal times for publishers bringing out new novels by D. H. Lawrence, and Caresse Crosbys' letters, as well as Lawrence's, show a strong concern about getting the novel safely into America. The difficulties which Lawrence had and was still having at this time with the civil authorities in both England and America over *Lady Chatterley's Lover* are well known. It should also be recalled that his manuscript of *Pansies* was seized by Scotland Yard who considered the poems "indecent and obscene" (January 1929. See CL, p. 1127). There was also the seizure and "trial" of Lawrence's paintings in the midst of their showing at a London gallery (July 1929). In some respects, 1929 was not a good year for Lawrence. But assuming that the Crosbys would remain undaunted and that they are not responsible for the omissions, who might have deleted the passages. Lawrence?

Lawrence could have deleted the passages in a stage prior to the page proofs, a stage closer to the actual typescript, i.e., the galleys. There is, however, no record in the correspondence of Lawrence's correcting galleys, and there are no surviving galleys recorded. Did Lawrence ever receive a set of galleys? It should be recalled that as late as 2 August 1929 Lawrence had not had even a definite commitment from the Crosbys. Sometime around 8 August, he must have received such a decision and also a set of page proofs, for he returned the "décors" and "corrected proofs" on 15 August. Mrs. Crosby replied on 27 August that she had received the decorations and the proofs and that she would be able "to send [Lawrence] an advance copy about the middle of September." There does not appear to have been a sufficient time gap—sufficient for printing, correcting and the necessary exchanging through the post—for a galley stage. I do not believe Lawrence ever received galleys. But the surviving *page proofs* indicate that Lawrence *did* correct them. How then could phrases extant in the author's manuscript but missing from the next stage, the page proofs, have been deleted *by the author without* a galley stage?

It might be suggested that Lawrence agreed to their omission when he met the Crosbys in Paris and first approached them with the possibility of their publishing the novel. But there is no evidence of this, and no mention in the letters of any necessary omissions. Indeed, there is much more evidence to suggest that the Crosbys had not even read the novel before Lawrence left Paris. I can find no method whereby the author could thus edit his own work. And when we consider the nature of the omissions, it is not very likely that Lawrence would have authorized them. These passages fall into two broad categories. First, there are passages of an explicit sexual nature and which are highly characteristic of Lawrence's narrative style. There is no conceivable reason why an author who had insisted on his right to a full expression of sexual matters in *Lady Chatterley's Lover* would eliminate such comparatively innocuous phrases as "penis" or "buttocks" or the sexual metaphor in "her bud" or "sad stones." Secondly, there are passages of a repetitive nature. I am consequently of the opinion that the deletions were made while the manuscript was in the hands of the Crosbys by them or by someone else in their publishing firm.

IX. TABLE OF VARIANTS
Compiled by Seamus Cooney

The following is a compilation of the variants between the Knopf and Heinemann texts currently in print (titled *The Man Who Died*) and the present edition. The text of the former is in roman type, that of the latter in italic. Variants in spelling, paragraphing, and punctuation have not been recorded.

PART 1

1 resplendent with arched and orange neck
   resplendent with an arched and orange neck

1a A saucy, flamboyant bird, that has already made
   A saucy, flamboyant bird, that had already made

2 Through all the long sleep
   Through all the long, long sleep

3 But now, something had returned to him,
   But now, something had returned him,

4 he leaned forward, in that narrow well of rock,
   he leaned forward, in that narrow cell of rock,

5 a slow squalor of limbs, yet he felt a certain compassion
   a slow squalor of limbs, and he felt a certain disgust

6 as if electricity had touched him
   as if a snake had touched him

7 The man addressed, with a sudden flicker of smile
   The man addressed, with a sudden flicker of life

8 You will have to go before a judge
   You too will have to go before a judge

9 through the inner doorway into the yard
   through the inner doorway to the yard

10 but fear made them compassionate
   but fear made them willing to serve

11 giving back a clumsy gentleness again
   giving back a clumsy service again

12 he said to them gently
   he said to them quietly

13 And then I shall go away for ever.
   And when I go away you will be paid.

14 They believed him at once
   They believed him really

15 The man who had died looked nakedly on life
   The man who had died looked nakedly onto life

16 And the cock, with the flat, brilliant
   And the cock, with a flat, brilliant

17 I was wrong to seek to lift it up. I was wrong
   I was wrong to seek to lift it up. It was wrong

18 So he saw the man, the peasant, with compassion
   So he saw the man, the peasant, with calm eyes

19 he saw a woman hovering by the tomb
   he saw a woman hovering [close] to the tomb
       (Forum text: he saw a woman hovering close to the tomb)

20 Then she reeled as if she would fall
   Then she went pale as if she would fall

21 now I can go about my business
   now I can go about my own business

22 My public life is over, the life of my self-importance. . . . And I know
   I wronged Judas, my poor Judas. For I have died
   My public life is over, the life of my conviction and my mission, the life
   of my self-importance. . . . And I know I wronged Judas, my poor Judas.
   Now I know. He died as I died, my poor Judas. For I have died

23 Yet I would embrace multitudes, I who have never truly embraced even

164

one. But Judas and the high priests saved me from my own salvation, and soon I can turn to my destiny like a bather in the sea at dawn, who has just come down to the shore alone.

Yet I would embrace multitudes, I who have never truly embraced even one woman, or one man. But Judas and the high priests delivered me from my own salvation, and I am no longer a lover of multitudes.

24 So Pilate and the high priests saved me from my own excessive salvation.
So Judas and the high priests snatched me from my own excessive giving.

25 Don't run to excess now in living, Madeleine.
Don't run to excess now in giving, Madeleine.

26 the female who had caught men at her will
the female who had caught men with her will

27 The cloud of necessity was on her, to be saved from the old, wilful Eve, who had embraced many men. . . . And that, too, is hard, and cruel to the warm body.
The cloud of necessity was on her, to be saved from the old, greedy self who had embraced many men . . . . and that too is vicious and cruel to the warm body.

28 The Messiah had not risen. The enthusiasm and the burning purity were gone
The Messiah had not risen. This was just a man. The enthusiasm and the burning purity were gone

29 "Where have you been?" she said.
"Where have you been, Master!" she said.

30 But he could not want her, though he felt gently towards her soft, crouching, humble body.
Bue he could not want her, though he felt troubled by her soft, crouching, humble body.

31 So he spoke a quiet, pleasant word to her and turned away. He could not touch the little, personal body, the little, personal life of this woman, nor in any other. He turned away from it without hesitation.
So he spoke a quiet, courteous word to her, and turned away.

32 Now he knew that he had risen for the woman, or women, who knew the greater life of the body, not greedy to give, not greedy to take, and with whom he could mingle his body. But having died, he was patient, knowing there was time, an eternity of time. And he was driven by no greedy desire, either to give himself to others, or to grasp anything for himself. For he had died.
Now he knew that he had risen for the greater life of the body, not greedy to give, not greedy to take, but moving towards the living being with whom he could mingle his body. Now, having died, he was patient, knowing there was time, an eternity of time. And he was driven by no greedy desire, either to give himself to others, or to grasp anything for himself. For he had died. And he knew how rare was the risen body, the twice-born limbs rare, rarer far than the twice-born spirit, which could house in greedy flesh.

33 because the peasant stood there in the little, personal body . . . . But the hope was cunning in him.
because the peasant stood there in the little, greedy body . . . . But the will was cunning in him.

34 beyond the little, narrow, personal life
beyond the little, narrow, greedy life

35 and have no connection, and mission or gospel is gone from me.
and have no connection, and my mission or gospel is gone from me.

36 And his need of men and women, his fever to have them
And his need of men and women, his fever to save them

37 touch between himself and the race of men
touch between himself and the race of man

38 How good it is to have fulfilled my mission
How glad I am, to have fulfilled my mission

39 the place where words can bite no more and the air
the place where words can bite and the air

40 Therefore he cut his hair and his beard after the right fashion, and smiled to himself.
Therefore he cut his hair and his beard after the right fashion, and moved slowly.

41 "Yes, for the time is come for me to return to men."
"Yea, for the time is come for me to return to men."

42 to be fulfilled in his own loneliness in the midst
to be fulfilled in his own aloneness in the midst

43 For previously he had been too much mixed up in it.
For previously he had been too much identified with it.

44 Yet I am apart! And life bubbles variously. Why should I have wanted
Yet I am apart! And life bubbles everywhere, in me, in them, in this, in that. But it bubbles variously. Why should I ever have wanted

45 For the body of my desire has died, and I am not in touch anywhere.
For the body of my desire has died, and I am not in touch any more.

46 So he smiled to himself, for a dangerous
So he was wary in himself, for a dangerous

47 "Yea!" he said laughing softly.
"Yea!" he said, mocking softly.

48 It was the mania of cities and societies
It was the mania of individuals, it was the mania of cities and societies

PART II

1 the little causeway of a rock
the little causeway of rock

2 yet far too quickly for anything dead
yet far too quick for anything dead

3 And in an instant he was covering her in the blind, frightened frenzy of a boy's first passion.
And in an instant he was in to her, covering her in the blind, frightened frenzy of a boy's first coition.

4 supporting the roof and open, spiky lotus-flowers
supporting the roof and the open, spiky lotus-flowers

5 a few grains of incense on a brazier
a few grains of incense on the brazier

166

6 the final clue to him, that alone could bring him really back to her. For she
   the final clue to him, the genitals that alone could bring him really back
   to her, and touch her womb. For she

7 Ah, come, a maid should open to the sun
   Ah come, a maid should open her bud to the sun

8 one of these rare, invisible suns
   one of those rare invisible suns

9 offers her soft, gold depths such as
   offers her soft, gold depth such as

10 But for the golden brief day-suns of show such as Anthony
   But for the golden brief-day suns of show, such as Anthony

11 So she had waited. For all the men
   So she had waited, but the bud of her womb had never stirred. For all
   the men

12 an inward meanness, an inadequacy. And Rome and Egypt
   an inward meanness, an inadequacy. And never once had her womb stirred
   its lotus bud, though the maleness of men had caressed the surface of her
   being like a pool. And Rome and Egypt

13 mystery. She had brought Isis
   mystery. So she brought Isis

14 "A slave will show you the shelter."
   "A slave shall show you the shelter."

15 to triumph in imparting the unpleasant news.
   to triumph in imparting this unpleasant news.

16 And in the pale skin of his feet
   And in the pale skin of the feet

17 but never had touched her with the flame-tip of life.
   but never had touched her on the yearning quick of her womb, with the
   flame-tip of life.

18 He had come back to life, but not the same life
   He had come back to life, but not to the same life

19 the dark figure of the man, sitting in that terrible stillness
   the dark figure of the man, sitting on the steps by the pink-and-blue pillar,
   sitting in that terrible stillness

20 she asked, with a hurried preoccupation of a priestess.
   she asked, with the hurried preoccupation of a priestess.

21 "Will you not look at Isis?"
   "Will you not look on Isis?"

22 He pried small shell-fish from the rocks
   He prised small shell-fish from the rocks

23 the westering sun on her nettled hair (Knopf only)
   the westering sun on her netted hair (as in Heinemann)

24 slaves were lifting small nets
   slaves were lifting the small nets

25 "Yes, if thou wilt heal me!"
   "Yea, if thou wilt heal me!"

26 The man who had died sat on at the foot of the tree
    But the man who had died sat on at the foot of the tree

27 where the man who had died was still sitting, inconspicuous
    where the man who had died still was sitting, inconspicuous

28 fat-shouldered slave rose, pallid in the shadow, with
    fat-shouldered slave rose, pallid in shadow, with

29 and the women slaves with the heaped baskets
    and the women-slaves with heaped baskets

30 So that he knew that her mother would
    So that he knew her mother would

31 At the same time he was haunted by the fear of
    At the same time he was haunted by fear of

32 And again he said to himself
    And he said again to himself

33 looking out on a gray darkness
    looking out on grey darkness

34 [entry deleted]

35 watched her slowly fan the brazier   (Knopf only)
    watched her softly fan the brazier   (as in Heinemann)

36 How sensitive and softly alive she is, with a life so different
    How sensitive and softly alive she is! How alive she is, with a life so different

37 Will you not take off your things?"
    Will you take off your things, and come to Isis?"

38 in her naïf priestess's absorption
    in her naïf priestess' absorption

39 It was here that his blood had left him, and his essential seed.
    It was here that his blood left him, and his water, and his essential seed.

40 felt his wounds crying aloud, and the deep places of his body
    felt his wounds crying aloud, and his bowels and the deep places of his body

41 "I am going to be warm again, and I am going to be whole!
    I am going to be flushed warm again, I am going to be whole!

42 Having chafed all his lower body with oil, having worked
    Having chafed all his lower body with oil, his belly, his buttocks, even the slain penis and the sad stones, having worked

43 in a power of living warmth, like the folds of a river.
    in a power of living warmth, like in the folds of a river.

44 and there was a stillness, and darkness
    and there was stillness and darkness

45 the girdle of the living woman slip down from him, the warmth and the glow slipped from him
    the girdle of the living woman slip from him, the warmth and the glow slipped down from him

46 hiding her face.
      Stooping, he laid
    hiding her face.
    He quivered, as the sun burst up in his body. Stooping he laid

47 Consuming desire, and the last thought
    consuming desire and a last thought

48 So he knew her, and was one with her.
    So he knew her, and was at one with her.

49 my atonement with you."
      And when they left the temple
    my atonement with you."
    And his desire flamed sunwise again, towards her, so he knew her
    again, and his bowels gloried in her. And as they lay in stillness, belly to
    belly, her bowels praised life.
    When they left the temple

50 shows where the dew touches
    shows where dew touches

51 the perfume of bean-field was in the air.
    the perfume of bean-fields was in the air.

52 But thou, do you watch
    But thou, do thou watch

53 "Not twice! They shall not now profane
    Not twice! They shall not twice lay hands on me. They shall not now
    profane

54 Stay with me on half the island, and I
    Stay with me on the half-island, and I

55 caught a whiff of flesh
    caught the whiff of flesh

56 the faint perfume of the Roman.
    the faint perfume from the Roman.

57 he said, in a clear voice:
    he said, in a small clear voice:

X. BIBLIOGRAPHY

Brett, Dorothy. *Lawrence and Brett*. London: Secker, 1933.

Brewster, Earl and Achsah. *D. H. Lawrence: Reminiscences and Correspond-ence*. London: Secker, 1934.

Brown, Curtis. *Contacts*. New York: Harper & Brothers, 1935

Chambers, Maria. "Afternoons in Italy with D. H. Lawrence." *Texas Quarterly*, 7 (Winter, 1964), 114-120.

Farmer, David Robb. "A Descriptive and Analytical Catalogue of the D. H. Lawrence Collection at the University of Texas at Austin." Unpublished dissertation. The University of Texas at Austin, 1970.

Ford, George H. *Double Measure*. New York: Norton, 1965.

Frazer, Sir James George. *The Golden Bough*, abridged edition. London: Mac-millan, 1971.

——. *Adonis, Attis, Osiris: Studies in the History of Oriental Religion.* 3rd ed., revised and enlarged. New York: University Books, 1961.

Friedman, Maurice. *To Deny Our Nothingness: Contemporary Images of Man.* New York: Dell, 1967.

Lawrence, D. H. *The Collected Letters of D. H. Lawrence.* Ed. Harry T. Moore. 2 vols. New York: Viking Press, 1962.

——. *Etruscan Places.* See *Mornings in Mexico and Etruscan Places.*

——. *The Letters of D. H. Lawrence.* Ed. Aldous Huxley. London: Heinemann, 1956.

——. *The Letters of D. H. Lawrence.* Ed. Diana Trilling. New York: Viking Press, 1947.

——. *Mornings in Mexico and Etruscan Places.* Harmondsworth, Middlesex: Penguin Books, 1967.

——. *Phoenix: The Posthumous Papers of D. H. Lawrence.* Ed. Edward McDonald. London, Heinemann, 1961.

——. *Phoenix II: Uncollected, Unpublished and Other Prose Works.* Eds. Warren Robert and Harry T. Moore. London: Heinemann, 1968.

——. *The Princess and Other Stories.* Ed. Keith Sagar. Harmondsworth, Middlesex: Penguin Books, 1971.

——. *The Quest for Rananim: D. H. Lawrence's Letters to S. S. Koteliansky, 1914-1930.* Ed. George J. Zytaruk. Montreal and London: McGill-Queen's University Press, 1970.

——. *St. Mawr and The Man Who Died.* New York: Vintage Books, 1953.

——. *The Selected Letters of D. H. Lawrence.* Ed. Richard Aldington. Harmondsworth, Middlesex: Penguin Books, 1950.

——. *Sons and Lovers: Text, Background, and Criticism.* Ed Julian Moynahan. New York: Viking Press, 1968.

——. "Unterwegs." *Die Neue Rundschau,* 45 (Band II, 1934), 702-717.

——. "The Unpublished Letters of D. H. Lawrence to Max Mohr." *T'ien Hsia Monthly,* 1 (August, 1935).

——. "The Unpublished Letters of D. H. Lawrence to Max Mohr." *T'ien Hsia Monthly,* 1 (September, 1935).

Lawrence, Frieda. *Not I, But the Wind. . . .* New York: Knopf, 1934.

Luhan, Mabel Dodge. *Lorenzo in Taos.* New York: Viking Press, 1934.

Moore, Harry T. *Poste Restante: A Lawrence Travel Calendar.* Berkeley and Los Angeles: University of California Press, 1956.

Murry, J. M. *Reminiscences of D. H. Lawrence.* London: Cape, 1933.

Roberts, Warren. *A Bibliography of D. H. Lawrence.* London: Rupert Hart-Davis, 1963.

Sagar, Keith. *The Art of D. H. Lawrence.* Cambridge: Cambridge University Press, 1966.

Tedlock, E. W., Jr. *The Frieda Lawrence Collection of D. H. Lawrence Manuscripts: A Descriptive Bibliography.* Albuquerque: University of New Mexico Press, 1948.

"In the face of formidable initial disadvantages and life-long delicacy, poverty that lasted for three-quarters of his life and hostility that survives his death, he did nothing that he did not really want to do, and all that he most wanted to do he did. He went all over the world, he owned a ranch, he lived in the most beautiful corners of Europe, and met whom he wanted to meet and told them that they were wrong and that he was right. He painted and made things and sang and rode. He wrote something like three dozen books, of which even the worst pages dance with life that could be mistaken for no other man's, while the best are admitted, even by those who hate him, to be unsurpassed. Without vices, with most human virtues, the husband of one wife, scrupulously honest, this estimable citizen yet managed to keep free of the shackles of civilization and the cant of literary cliques. He would have laughed lightly and cursed venomously in passing at the solemn owls—each one secretly chained by the leg. . . . . To do his work and lead his life in spite of them took some doing, but he did it, and long after they are forgotten, sensitive and innocent people—if any are left— will turn Lawrence's pages and know from them what sort of a rare man Lawrence was."

—Catherine Carswell